Advance praise for Arn...
Leo@fergusrules.com

If ever a writer's reputation can be established just with one published work, this one's it. In a nutshell it's one helluva novel: vibrant, vital, energetic, polished, quick, funny, rich, imaginative, sad and powerful and original. It's also something most first novels aren't: deeply intelligent, eminently readable, highly exotic, and practically flawless. It's as if all of Mr. Tangherlini's previous unpublished fiction was a sharpening of the stick for this one. I couldn't put the darn thing down and I immediately knew I'd soon be reading it again. Dialog, characterizations, story, structure, all work remarkably well together, producing the genuine article and a work of art. What I also found unusual was how he was able to master a foreign culture and incorporate it into so contemporary a novel. The reader should prepare for a highly charged, entertaining and engrossing experience, and before you know it, damn, the book's over with.

—Stephen Dixon

Leo@fergusrules.com reminds me of the novels I loved as a kid, Narnia, Alice, Phantom Tollbooth—books that are secret gardens, with pages that whisper of other worlds. And yet, because of its literary allusions (Borges, Eco, Dante et. al.) and challenging ideas, it definitely belongs in the adult section. The narrator, a hormone-addled teen girl, dons a virtual-reality visor and goes off on a heroic journey that would make Joseph Campbell's head spin. On the way, she encounters mythological beasts from her Philippine grandmother's stories, a gaggle of mall rats, and a Zamboni ice-cleaner that's a portal to another dimension. *Leo@fergusrules.com* is a bit like a virtual-reality visor itself—disorienting, new, and utterly diverting.

—Pagan Kennedy

Leo@fergusrules.com

Leo@fergusrules.com

a novel by
Arne Tangherlini

with an afterword by
Pagan Kennedy

The Leapfrog Press
Wellfleet, Massachusetts
www.leapfrogpress.com

Library of Congress Cataloging-in-Publication Data
Tangherlini, Arne E., 1960–
    Leo@fergusrules.com : a novel / by Arne Tangherlini. — 1st ed.
    p.   cm.
    ISBN 0-9654578-7-7
    I.   Title.
PS3570.A527L46   1999
813' .54—dc21   99-19411
                                                     CIP

Book design and typography by Erica L. Schultz.

Printed in the United States of America

10 9 8 7 6 5 4 3 2 1

Published in the United States by
The Leapfrog Press
P.O. Box 1495
Wellfleet, MA 02667-1495, USA
www.leapfrogpress.com

Distributed in the United States by
Consortium Book Sales and Distribution
St. Paul, Minnesota 55114

For Nastasia,
Betrayed by Christopher Robin

CHAPTER ONE

I insist on durian. I love the sweet taste of the meat, and the rotten cheese stench of the skin keeps the curious from my room. I have the maid bring it up twice a day and leave it outside my door. When you're chasing Genghis Khan across the Tekla Makhan or gouging the eye from a Cyclops, the last thing you need is to be called down for supper—especially when it's a plate of hard rice and chicken overcooked in vinegar and soy sauce.

I wrote that in my journal ten months ago when I arrived in Manila. At the time, I was battling my grandmother, Lola Flor, who wanted to impose her medieval notions of order on me. In her house, every day was regulated according to the canonical hours of a monastery: breakfast was served at lauds, just as the sun rose; I left for school at prime; we recited the rosary right after I came home from school at none; we sat down to supper at vespers; and at complin Lola marched around the house turning out the lights. At school, she wanted me to listen for the bells of St. Andrew's and take my lunch when terce sounded, but that meant eating during math class. I tried it once just to see what would happen. I'd no sooner unwrapped my chicken wings than Mrs. Siew sent me to the principal's office.

Lola still lives in a Philippines that's been buried under concrete and limestone for fifty years. She believes that the world is inhabited by spirits, and she's full of advice on how to handle witches, ghosts, little people called *duwende,* and

1

monsters called *tikbalang*. After supper, she'll take hold of my hand and, whispering in a mixture of Tagalog and Waray (the language of her province, Samar), give me all sorts of useless advice: "Don't walk across the rice fields without watching for the homes of the *duwende*. If you come across a small mound in the field, that is probably home to a *duwende*. Before you pass by, make sure you say your apologies. Kneel down by the home of the *duwende* and speak in a soft, respectful voice. Tell the *duwende* where you are going. Be very polite and honest and he will not bother you. Never pass under a mango tree in the nighttime. The *tikbalang* are hungry for the flesh of young boys."

The first few times she spoke of the *tikbalang*'s eating habits, I interrupted to remind her that I am a girl. But after a while I let it slide. A lot of people get confused when they meet me. I wear my hair short, shaved above the ears in the style they used to call a fade. My pants and t-shirts are baggy. Not that it matters. I'm about as shapely as a soda can.

I learned a long time ago that you can use people's confusion to your advantage. If you keep them guessing, they're never sure how to treat you. If you're smart, you make them treat you the way you want to be treated. Having Lola think of me as a boy didn't hurt at all: as long as she was confused, she stopped worrying about the way I dressed, whether I helped with the dishes, cleaned my room, or learned to cook. Instead, I read to her from the Bible and listened to her stories. And sometimes, when she was in the mood, we danced.

"You will recognize the *tikbalang* as a big black horse with red eyes who smokes a pipe and walks upright like a man," she explained. "If you see him, run away. Don't turn around to see if he's chasing. Run only. You can gain control of the *tikbalang* by plucking out three of his hairs and leaping onto his back. Never try to do this. He will be very angry if you try and fail. Never fall asleep under a mango tree even in the daytime. If you do, you may never wake up again."

Even though I was skeptical, I listened to everything Lola told me. I felt sorry for her. Like me, she'd been abandoned by her family. Some of the things she told me were funny. She said that I am going to be rich because my second toe is longer than my big toe, which she warned me not to show anyone: otherwise, the blessing would be taken away. She said that my aura was blue, but that it was surrounded by a yellow cloud. This meant that I was really a good person, but all of my troubles were making me act as if I was bad.

I don't believe in auras or any other superstitious mumbo-jumbo. Lola Flor said those things to make me feel good about myself. But the fact is I'm rotten to the core, and I have evidence to prove it. In my fourteen years of existence I have attended seventeen different schools. My father is an engineer who specializes in earthquake-proofing. His expertise is in demand wherever people build skyscrapers, but that is only a partial explanation for my inconstancy. In Lima, I was thrown out of kindergarten for arguing with the teacher about the intentions of Jack when he climbed up the beanstalk. She said he wanted to take care of his mother, but I insisted that he was just a common thief. For three months, I wouldn't talk to her about anything else. I kept interrupting her to bring up new scraps of evidence. Finally, she sent me to see the school psychologist, and he recommended that I find another school. In third grade, in the middle of the Zambian rains, I lit a classmate's desk on fire. In Baltimore, I hacked into the school computer and fixed the schedule so that everyone had to fit eight classes into seven periods. It took the guidance counselors three weeks to sort it out. In the meantime, the teachers went on strike and the principal was transferred to the central office.

I can hardly remember why I was thrown out of the other schools. My presence is provocative. I start fights with a glance or a word. Sometimes I feel like I'm hovering outside of my body, watching and listening as the words—cruel, quick smart-bombs that always find their targets—are launched rapid-fire from my mouth.

To make matters worse, my aim is always best when the victim is someone I admire. I'd been in Manila two weeks—having resolved to do better in eighth grade, for Lola's sake at least—when I opened fire on a classmate. Like me, Bri (he pronounces it like the cheese) is mestizo (he calls us "mongrels"); only instead of being Filipino-Italian-American, he's part Danish, part Korean, part Brazilian (which also makes him African, Tolmec, and Russian-Jewish, he says). He's handsome in an odd, unbalanced way. It's as if all of the different features haven't quite figured out how they're going to blend yet. His hair is an unruly mop of curls, dark brown at the roots and yellow at the tips, like that of a fisherman or someone else who lives in the sun. His eyes are lucid brown, pale and clear as bottle glass. He is gangly, boneless, protean: he occupies a desk as a cat might, curling about it, making his shape conform to its contours. His mind is what impresses me most, though: he speaks six languages and programs in twice as many. He solves five-step algebraic problems in his head. He reads hexadecimal code like you or I might read Dr. Seuss.

None of the other girls in our class seem to be interested in him. I suppose they think he's a nerd. But school is not the only thing he's good at: he's the goalie on the soccer team and he plays cello in the orchestra.

Anyway, Bri had recited "Who Goes with Fergus," a poem by William Butler Yeats, in Humanities class. I was amazed, because Fergus is my name in Apeiron. I took the name from an Irish king after I defeated him in battle. I

made his castle my home; I used his coat-of-arms; I even
made myself look like him. Anyway, I loved the poem and
the way Bri recited it, especially the last few lines:

For Fergus rules the brazen cars
And rules the shadows of the wood,
And the white breast of the dim sea,
And all dishevelled wandering stars.

It reminded me of adventure and loneliness and something
else that I couldn't name. After the recitation, we were each
supposed to say something we liked about the poem or the
delivery. But when I opened my mouth, trash came out.

"Fairgoose," I said, exaggerating his Danish accent.
"What's all the fuss about a fair goose?"

Everyone in the class laughed, and as usual, Michael
Contreras fell off his chair.

Bri just smiled at me and shook his head as if to say,
"You'll have to do better than that."

Our teacher, Dr. Jack, didn't take it as well. Though he's
usually as brown as the coffee beans from his native Batangas,
he turned red all the way up to his bald spot, so that even his
beard seemed to glow. He grabbed me by the shoulder and
dragged me out into the hallway. He was breathing heavily
and squinting as if it hurt him to look at me. He shook me,
not roughly but firmly, as if he were trying to wake me up.

"Don't you have any notion of mystery or beauty," he
said. "Weren't you even a little bit moved?"

I felt like I was going to get sick. Dr. Jack was my favorite
teacher. His class was challenging, and he wasn't condescend-
ing. We studied ancient civilizations; we read Lao Tzu,
Confucius, Homer, Euripides, Plato, and Sappho; we had vocabulary words like *lucubration, micturate, satyriasis,* and *bor-*
borygmus. We studied logic and grammar, and we learned to

recite poetry by heart. I wanted to tell him how I felt. I wanted to tell him that I loved the poem, and that I had only made fun of Bri because I didn't want to cry in front of my classmates. Instead I just stood there stupidly, looking down at my shoes.

CHAPTER TWO

Lola Flor had her accident during the first week of January. Going to confession one Friday evening, she was sideswiped by a speeding jeepney—one of those giant aluminum cans painted in electric colors that crowd the streets of Manila, spewing out passengers and a cloying fog of diesel. With a hip and shoulder broken, she was confined to her room, and though she had never been able to control me, from then on I was left entirely to my own devices.

The devices were a payoff, guilt-gifts from my mom and stepfather. The headgear is standard issue, nothing more, nothing less than you'd find at any arcade. I had a full body suit and motion control, of course. My computer was fast—faster than the best machines at school—but there were faster systems on the market. What mattered most was the interface. Through my modem and a dedicated line, I was linked directly to Apeiron. Let them think the phone bill was so high because I was chatting with all my old friends in the States. When I was home, I was online to Apeiron.

Even if they knew about Apeiron, most kids talked like it was just another game environment. They flew through, strafed a village, killed a dragon or two, made love to a prince or princess, and then they'd complain that there was no score: you didn't gain hit-points or collect little treasures. But most kids are stupid. They don't see that games get boring. Playing a game is like riding a conveyor belt. After a while, you know exactly what's going to come at you. If you practice your moves enough and if you concentrate, you'll always win and move up to the next level. Winning at the next level usually requires more skill, more practice, more concentration—but the difference is in degree and not in kind.

Some players said that Apeiron was an alternate world just as valid as the one inhabited by our parents, our classmates, our teachers, principals, scientists, and beauticians. I met players and characters in Apeiron who argued, almost desperately, that it was more valid, more complete, more consistent. The spiritualists believed that after the coming apocalypse, only the few, the initiates of Apeiron, would survive. Cynics, on the other hand, maintained that Apeiron was a mistake—that it was an experiment gone haywire. They told the story that Apeiron was created by a graduate student at Cornell who threw himself into a gorge instead of acknowledging his mistake and erasing it while he could. Still others claimed that Apeiron was nothing more than a museum or a giant library; they attributed it to a mad encyclopedist at the Library of Congress or the Biblioteca Nacional in Buenos Aires obsessed with compiling all of human knowledge and experience in one system.

As far as I know, Apeiron was an environment designed to replace games with something more challenging and satisfying. There was no legal way of interfacing with Apeiron. You had to sneak in. By definition, all players in Apeiron were hackers. Several commercial game environments had back doors—walls you could breech, sewers you could swim through. At the border, you had to give a password, but getting one didn't take much skill, just a bit of persistence. I found a few when I was lurking in the system files of a mainframe in Arlington, Virginia.

Apeiron was not a place. Like those plants that entwine themselves in their host trees until they are inseparable and you cannot kill one without killing the other, Apeiron lived on the network. The information that allowed Apeiron to exist was not stored in a single machine. Apeiron was a parasite: it virtualized the memory of the entire network. It was the missing matter in the electronic universe. Apeiron was terrifying and beautiful. Apeiron was irresistible. Whenever I made a fool of myself in school or at home, I went to Apeiron to start over.

CHAPTER THREE

At the end of the narrow valley that borders the River Po, nestled in a glade of oak and beech trees, stood a medieval monastery with fortified walls and fields all around it. On my way to other parts of Apeiron, I loved to swoop down close and strafe the monks as they worked in the fields. I didn't think this amusement caused any lasting damage, because each time I flew over, the same monks were back in the same fields harvesting the same ripe yellow stalks of wheat. I was not especially entertained by the way the monks ran screaming from the fiery fields or splattered when I hit them, spewing bits of brain and guts on the ground. But there was one fat, bearded monk, with a head completely bald except for a wreath of white hair encircling his ears, who made the visit worth my while. He would run from the monastery shaking his fist and screaming Italian oaths at the sky.

"Disgraziato! Maleducato! Imbecille!" he would shout.

I do not know why I found this so amusing. Maybe it was just that he seemed to take his role so seriously. I had the sense that he was genuinely outraged—that he honestly believed that I was doing something wrong. Unlike the monks in the field, who would always be harvesting their corn, this monk, I began to imagine, had a life of his own in Apeiron.

On the first day of Easter vacation, I strafed the fields again. While I was watching him, trying to decipher the curses that streamed from his lips, I lost control of my jet and crashed into the forest. In Apeiron, I wear a full suit of fireproof armor imported from Uqbar (one of the best commercial game environments), so the damage to my cyberbody was minimal. But as soon as I'd leaped from the flaming hulk, the fat priest was on me like an overweight leopard pouncing on a meal. His breath smelled of garlic, onions, and wine, which was odd because I'd never noticed smells before in Apeiron.

I trained my revolver on him and ran a scan to determine whether he was a player or just a character. I have an LED display in my headgear that tells me about the creatures I meet—whether to attack or take evasive action and how to go about it. Maybe the hardware was damaged in the crash, because my scan of the monk came up blank. This had only happened once before, when I had gotten into a bind with Pallas Athena, the Greek goddess of wisdom. The scanner had gone haywire, someone explained to me later, because her memory and powers are infinite. Picking a fight with her would be like picking a fight with the entire network.

I did not have the sense that this fat, halitotic monk was in a class with Pallas Athena, so I opened fire. The bullets went right through him, and he continued panting and wiping his brow with a dirty handkerchief, as if he hadn't noticed.

In Apeiron, I am Fergus, six-foot-4-inches, 267 pounds, and a black belt in three martial arts. When Fergus hits people, they drop like empty book bags. I aimed a spin-kick at his jaw, but it was like striking air. I threw a punch at his swollen gut, but again nothing happened.

"Who are you?" I asked him at last, when he seemed to have recovered his breath. "Are you a player, or are you just a character?"

"Not a player, not a character," he answered. "I am Fra Umberto. I was once a man, and my parents were Piedmontese, from Alessandria, a village outside of Turin. But that is not even true. I am a shadow of a shadow. Try all your weapons on me." He tucked his handkerchief into his pocket and spread his hands wide. "I exist neither in time nor space.

I am one of the illusions of man's greatest creation, just like everything you see." Then he chuckled, so his belly bounced underneath the habit. "Look at the fields you just strafed."

I looked. The monks were back at work. There was no sign of carnage anywhere.

"Big deal," I said. "They're only characters. I could come back again in a week, strafe them, and they'd be reconstituted. I could reset now, get in my plane, fly over and destroy them again. Nothing would change."

"That's right. You have no effect on Apeiron. You are less than a shadow of a shadow."

This annoyed me. "I could set the woods on fire."

"Indeed."

"I could blow up your monastery."

"You could do many things, but none of them would have any effect on Apeiron."

"So why do you get so angry whenever I strafe the fields?"

"I get angry at your stupidity and ignorance. I get angry because you use man's greatest creation as a playground instead of trying to learn from it."

"What is it you want me to learn?"

"It wouldn't be learning if I told you beforehand."

He sounded like Dr. Jack—too mysterious for his own good. I'd told Dr. Jack about Apeiron once, and he'd called it a waste of time. "I have a teacher who says that there's nothing to be learned in Apeiron. He says I should stick to books," I said.

"Your teacher is right."

"He says the problem with Apeiron is that it contains too much information, that it doesn't distinguish what is important from what is drivel."

"You should listen to your teacher." Fra Umberto pushed the spectacles up his nose. "Apeiron will only confuse you. The principles governing existence here are entirely different from the ones that govern your world. Here there is neither time nor space. All moments in history are simultaneous—Medieval Italy, Tutankhamen's Egypt, Chou Dynasty China, Babylon. Apeiron is not a playground. It was created for seekers. It is both a warehouse of knowledge (a vast interactive encyclopedia if you will) and a laboratory for experiments. Scholars are free to roam and explore as they wish. Apeiron was never intended to be a playground for hooligans in fighter planes: there are plenty of commercial environments that provide such opportunities."

"I thought you said that Apeiron is free."

"It is indeed. And that may be its greatest flaw."

"In what sense?"

Fra Umberto inhaled through his nose and squinted at me, as if he was examining an unfamiliar dish, trying to decide whether or not to eat. "Recently, bits of information have been dropping out of Apeiron. We don't know how the information is lost, but we've discovered where it goes. There seems to be a pit—an electronic black hole if you will—between Apeiron and the network. We call it a pit because things just seem to fall in. We don't really know what it is. The disappearances are hardly systematic: many of them go unnoticed. At first it was just bits of code, data, descriptions, dates, words, the image of a flower or animal. But the effects have been disastrous. Some years ago, Einstein was introduced to teach us about relativity, but lately you'll find he spends his days playing dice with Shakespeare or gossiping with Marilyn Monroe about the Kennedy brothers."

"Then he isn't really Einstein," I said.

He nodded. "Of course not. He was never really Einstein, but at least he was not a gambler. I suspect that the designers of Apeiron made a fatal mistake when they tried to include everything. They forgot that a system cannot be both complete and consistent."

Fra Umberto cleared his throat. "Recently we've lost one of our young scholars. You might even know him," he said and reached into the pocket of his hassock, searching for something.

I had heard about this pit before. Players called it Dløn. It was supposed to be even more ambitious and mysterious than Apeiron. While Apeiron was an alternate world, Dløn was an entire universe. Mystics spoke about it as a sort of Holy Grail. They believed that Dløn was the source of tremendous power and incalculable wisdom. From what I'd heard, you couldn't set out for Dløn; you could only get there by chance. As the monk fumbled in his pocket, I wondered if he was going to present me with my chance.

"Here," he said, and he handed me a piece of cardboard that was badly wrinkled from having been in his pocket. "I cut this from a milk carton the other day."

The carton bore the familiar caption, "Have you seen this child?" The face in the picture was Bri's.

"Is this a joke?" I said.

Fra Umberto snatched the picture again. "I don't think there's anything funny about a missing boy," he said. But there was something about the way he cocked his head and squinted at me that made me think that he was trying not to laugh at me.

"How can he be missing in Apeiron?"

"Do you know him?"

"Yes."

"Are you responsible for his presence here?"

I mumbled, "Maybe."

I knew it was possible. For almost four years, I've been keeping a journal. I started doing it so I wouldn't forget people when I moved. I'd write about them and scan in pictures; sometimes, I'd even record their voices. I had a whole file on Bri.

It might sound weird, but after the poem incident, Bri had decided to become my friend. Somehow, he'd gotten my e-mail address (leo@fergusrules.com), and sent me a message. It was really nasty—and funny. He wrote in French, Italian, English, and two or three dialects of Filipino, making fun of my clothes, my voice, my eyes, and my ideas. He said I shouldn't wear hip-hop pants because my legs are already too stubby. He called my hairstyle antediluvian. He said my complexion is the color of *tae-tae*—which is Waray for diarrhea—even though his is a shade darker, with red tints instead of my yellows and greens. He continued discussions that had started in class. He said that I was stupid for liking Odysseus—he was a murderer and a sex fiend who depended on a goddess for everything. "Where would he be," Bri wrote, "without the help of Pallas Athena?"

In school, we ignored each other. If our eyes happened to meet, one of us would look away. We sat on opposite sides of the room, and he complained if Dr. Jack put us in the same group for a project. But we sent each other messages every day. My file on Bri consisted mostly of messages I'd copied into my journal and some photos I'd scanned from old yearbooks.

After a while, Bri became my comrade in arms when I traveled to Apeiron. To amuse ourselves, we fought battles with Chin Shih Huangti, Julius Caesar, Napoleon, and King Xerxes. One day we fought for them, the next time we were against. We rode horses, camels, elephants. We lived the nomadic life of Genghis Khan, sleeping in yurts and quenching our thirst with the sweat of our brows or the blood of our mares. We ambushed merchants along the Silk Road and made fortunes trading stolen goods in Venice and Genoa.

We appeared when least expected, armed with Uzis, rocket launchers, lasers. When Perseus came to cut off Medusa's head, we sent him packing. We freed the Trojan women from the clutches of sly Odysseus and the Greeks. We led the Dravidian charge to retake Mohenjo-Daro from the Aryans. We helped Cetshwayo drive the British out of Zululand. We taught Spartacus how to use heavy artillery.

In real life nothing changed. At school he didn't speak to me, and his e-mails remained insulting. But in Apeiron we drank from the same cup and ate from the same plate. We crossed the Andes and the Himalayas. We sailed up the Nile to its source. We forded rivers and slept under the stars in glacial fields of wild flowers. We went into battle shoulder to shoulder. No one could attack me from behind because he was always there to protect me. We never argued, never teased each other, never fought. We were Enkidu and Gilgamesh. We were Rama and Laksmana. We were friends.

About four months ago, right after New Years, Bri backed out of the partnership. He didn't say anything. He just stopped coming to Apeiron. Oddly enough, this happened on the same day that my journal, including my file on Bri, disappeared from my hard drive. I don't know how it happened or where it went. I'd been meaning to copy it all onto a disk for a long time, but I'd just never gotten around to it. I was sure it had just been erased somehow, but now I didn't know.

"He's not missing *in* Apeiron. He's missing *from* Apeiron," Fra Umberto said.

"What's the difference?"

"You wouldn't understand."

"Is it bad?"

Fra Umberto shook his head, and a huge bead of sweat crawled like a beetle from his forehead to the tip of his nose. "Terrible."

It was ridiculous to believe that Bri was really in danger. No doubt Fra Umberto, or whoever was using him, had taken the picture from my hard drive. But I liked the idea of going on a quest to save Bri. Maybe I would find out how he really felt about me. Or maybe I'd have a chance to recover my journal. Either way, I saw Dløn as the next step. Now I wouldn't be playing games anymore.

"Can I do anything to help him?" I asked, trying to sound nonchalant.

Fra Umberto scratched his nose as if distracted. "You have to come as yourself," he mumbled. "You can't have any special powers or abilities. No jets, no scanners, no fireproof armor, no karate, no kick-boxing, no disguises. No Uqbarian gadgets of any sort. Present yourself at the gate of the monastery unarmed and on foot. Make sure you've locked yourself into Apeiron for at least thirty-six hours. Any less and you may never return from the pit. The journey is a rough one. Hellish, I'd say. There's no guarantee you'll find him or that you'll survive if you do."

CHAPTER FOUR

After vespers on Good Friday, Lola Flor locked herself into her room to pray, having left directions with the maids that she was not to be disturbed until Easter Sunday morning. She would live for thirty-six hours on rice and water (a Filipino fast will always have rice; it's not cheating, just a practical matter, like the need to go to the bathroom). She would hallow herself in her room, which had nothing in it but a bed, a crucifix, and a poster of a monk amid a peaceful stratum of fields, with Latin verses of the Hours curled in gold against the sky, and in the distance, without perspective, a stained-glass monastery, an ungainly, poorly executed image, given the rigor of detail spent on the shimmering of the sheaves. The poster was a souvenir, I believe, from her trip to Lourdes and the Vatican, paid for by my mother in lieu of going with her. Whenever Lola opened her door, you saw the monk on her wall, his arms raised in what seemed more like outrage than devotion, abjuring some kind of infamy amid the fields.

No one dared cross Lola's room when she was in this state.

I was left to my usual devices.

Somehow, in that low hour, during the still, maudlin hours of Lenten silence, I found it comforting to imagine Lola in her world. I imagined her soul was as tranquil and ordered as the illuminated fields in those pictures of French manorial life. Row upon row of gilded agrarian green, sheaves of wheat bowed stiffly in schematic curls. Such was the state of her inner life—an etched medieval emblem, symbolizing grace or the banal delights of spiritual toil.

Outwardly, Lola had the musculature of a peasant and the suspicious eyes of a rice miller. She had once owned a warehouse in Samar and knew the ways of deceit; even while she spent her days counting the mysteries on her rosary, the servants were terrified of her, as if she could see them measuring out spoonfuls of Nestlé creamer into their coffee, which they did surreptitiously, trying not to make a sound. During the high days of Lent, they made sure I was safely in my room, and they closed all the shutters of the house. And then they got ready for sleep.

Through the bars on my windows, I could see the moon rising over the neighbor's mango tree and the lights going out in the office buildings of the financial district half a mile away. The village was quiet, except for the barking of dogs and the occasional distant rumble of a jeepney. A group of girls in dark dresses hurried past the house, and then the street was empty.

With his chair propped against the gate and his shotgun cradled like a kitten in his arms, the guard Emman was asleep. My stepfather's paranoia provides Emman this life of ease. Though he wants nothing to do with me, my stepfather is terrified that someone is going to kidnap me. He considers me an investment. That's why he is never reluctant to supply me with gadgets. When I got into trouble in Baltimore, he took great pride in the havoc I'd created in the school's computer system. I think he imagines that someday, I'll help him to recoup all the money he has spent on my mother.

Emman, of course, is useless. When he's not sleeping, he's eating or bothering the maids. The village already employs a squadron of guards that patrols the streets and stops every car at the gate. Anyway, it's ridiculous to think that anyone would want to kidnap me. Sometimes I imagine that

Emman and the others are really there to keep me from getting out and seeing the world. Sometimes I think that's what really frightens my stepfather.

Earlier, Chuki, one of the maids, had knocked at my door and called my name. Without answering, I waited for the sound of her flipflops slapping on the stairs before opening the door. She'd left behind a tray with a pitcher of water and two small durian. I peeled them slowly, letting the room fill up with the stench. Waiting for darkness, I ate the delicate white meat of both fruits—patiently, systematically—like a vulture picking at carrion.

It took me several hours to find my way to the monastery. I was unaccustomed to walking in Apeiron. I kept getting lost in the woods, and after a while my boots began to chafe my heels. I was thinking about resetting and flying in, but then I remembered I'd locked myself in for thirty-six hours. Anyway, you have to be at least six feet tall to fly an Uqbarian jet, and the truth is in boots I'm barely 4'10".

When I arrived at the monastery, Fra Umberto opened the gate before I could knock. "I thought there would be more to you," he said, chuckling so his eyes became squinty.

When I didn't answer, he took me by the arm and led me down a dark and narrow passageway. I thought it was strange that I could feel his touch when before my punches had passed right through him, but I was too nervous to say anything. His hold was firm and steady like Dr. Jack's. We crossed a cobblestoned courtyard and entered a massive building made of dark mossy stones. After passing through a tall door with a stained glass window on the transom, we found ourselves in a large, airy room. The walls were covered with book cases, strange paintings, and mirrors that created the illusion that the room went on forever and contained an infinite number of books.

In a corner where there were no mirrors, Fra Umberto sat down behind a huge desk that was nearly buried in papers, books, and magazines. He motioned for me to take a seat across from him, then his eye fell on the page of a book that lay open before him. He looked tired and distracted. His habit was wrinkled and stained with some green, powdery substance, and beneath his eyes the skin seemed to sag like a rhino's. He kept looking at the book as if searching for something he intended to read to me. In the meantime, his eyebrows seemed to dance on his forehead like giant caterpillars, each with a will and a music of its own.

"Well," he said, at last, looking at me over his glasses. "Take a look around. This is supposed to be the greatest library of all times. It contains every book that was ever written—or it did." He pushed his glasses up his nose. "Last time we met, I told you about things disappearing into the pit."

"Books?" I said.

"If only. No, none of the books have disappeared. Pages have disappeared, illustrations, passages. I will open a play and look for a speech that I have committed to memory, and it simply won't be there any more. Sometimes a new speech will have been put in its place, or a word or two will have been altered. Sometimes, the speech will just be gone. But there is never any evidence in the books. They are not real books. You don't have to cross out a word to change it or tear out a page to make it vanish. You don't even have to visit the library to manipulate its contents." Fra Umberto took off his glasses and rubbed his eyes with his fists.

"After a while, you begin to doubt your own judgment. You wonder how many of the books have been tampered with. You find yourself checking over and over. And you start to believe that everything is contaminated."

Fra Umberto slammed the cover of the book on his desk and rose with a sudden burst of energy. "I know you haven't come here to listen to my problems. You've come to help a friend. Let me warn you again that it won't be easy."

I was anxious to show him that I wasn't afraid. "How will we get there?" I blurted.

"The descent is simple," he said. "We can enter the pit from the monastery. Indeed, we can enter it from this room. But to retrace your steps and return to the upper air—that's the difficulty." Fra Umberto sighed. "Do you think you're ready?"

I nodded.

Fra Umberto pointed at a painting that hung on a far wall of the room. "You see the painting over there that looks like a random arrangement of colors and fragments from disconnected images? Stare at it until it begins to swirl, until you begin to see a three-dimensional image. Don't resist when you start to fall. That's the entry to the pit."

I had tried staring at those pictures a thousand times before and had never once succeeded in seeing what everyone else saw in them. I would have told Fra Umberto, but I was too embarrassed. I stared for a while without any luck; then Fra Umberto spoke, as if he'd read my mind.

"If you can't make it work, stare at your reflection in the glass. Be patient; gradually you'll find your way."

I do not like mirrors. They remind me of things I'd rather forget. I have my mother's eyes, and they say that is my best feature. From Father, I get my curls, which are the reason my hair is always a mess. My skin is the color of coffee with a drop of milk and a tablespoon of olive oil in it—not light enough to be light, not dark enough to be dark; in the sun, I turn a weird greenish shade of brown—an unfortunate admixture of tints from both sides of the family. My nose is my ugliest trait. I have a huge Italian nose (Lola Flor says it's "classical") attached to a sunken Filipino bridge: a Dolomite rising from the Central Luzon Plain. That day it was particularly gruesome, for at the tip of that massive chunk of cartilage and skin, I'd sprouted a bulbous red zit.

CHAPTER FIVE

Suddenly I was spinning through the air, flipping and turning, as if on a roller coaster that had jumped its track. A sharp keening like electric guitar feedback or the sound of a hundred kids swinging on rusty swings pierced my ears, and I had to close my eyes to still the bright kaleidoscope of colored shapes that was tumbling at me. After falling for several minutes, I landed on a muddy slope by the edge of a stinking brown river. All along the shore were shanties made of scraps of wood and rusted tin, cardboard, street signs, and plastic bags. On the roofs of these rickety buildings, in the doorways, through the cracks in the walls, I saw children staring at me with huge hungry eyes.

Fra Umberto, holding his habit so it wouldn't drag in the mud, stood haggling with a scrawny little boatman at the water's edge. They spoke a language I did not understand, but I could tell from their gestures that Fra Umberto wanted him to take us across the river, and that the boatman wanted more money than the priest was willing to pay. At last, Fra Umberto pulled the picture of Bri from his pocket and waved it in front of the boatman's face. After studying the picture for a while, the boatman nodded gravely and mumbled something to Fra Umberto. Crouching, holding onto the gunwales, the fat priest crept into the little boat. He did not signal for me to follow until he was comfortably seated on the floor.

The boat was a narrow and whippy dug-out canoe, made in the style of a Filipino fishing *bangka,* with bamboo outriggers jutting from both sides. We floated fifty yards downstream before the boatman was able to start the engine. The surface of the water glowed with oily rainbows. I was staring at one of these when suddenly a boy's face broke the surface of the water. He squinted at me, as if trying to remember where he'd seen me before. Then suddenly I knew him. Every morning on the way to school, at the intersection of Buendia and Makati Avenues, he would put his face up to the tinted glass of the car to beg and stare at me.

Once I gave him a peso. The coin was still in my hand when the driver Mang Joe began rolling up the window. He yelled at me all the way to school. He said there was no point in giving money to beggars, because it only encouraged them to keep begging. Now I searched my pockets, but I had nothing in them. The boy was reaching out to take hold of the outrigger when the boatman smacked him on the head with his paddle. As quickly as he had appeared, the boy sank below the surface.

Frantic, I pulled at the sleeve of Fra Umberto's habit.

"Why did he do that?" I asked.

"He's not a real child," Fra Umberto said. "He's a character, like the monks you used to strafe. Don't worry about it."

"But I know him."

"You couldn't possibly know him. You only think you know him," Fra Umberto scolded.

Now we were speeding towards the opposite bank, where towering black factory buildings stood out against a murky yellow sky. Hundreds of naked children swam in the viscous muck that poured from the great cement pipes feeding the river. Directly ahead of us, above the largest of the pipes, a giant red and white neon sign blinked a familiar and reassuring message: "It's the Real Thing." Without slowing down, we sailed right into the mouth of this pipe—into a tunnel that must have been thirty meters high and forty meters across.

A few hundred meters in, the boatman deposited us on a little platform on the left side of the tunnel. After Fra Umberto had paid him, he sped away without a word to either of us, the clatter of his motor echoing for several minutes after his disappearance. From the platform, a narrow spiral staircase rose towards the ceiling of the tunnel.

"Well," Fra Umberto said, rubbing his hands. "What are you waiting for?"

"Should I go first?"

"There's no guarantee I'll fit. And even if I do, what if I slip? You wouldn't want me to fall on you."

The stairway did not stop at the ceiling of the tunnel but continued rising into a narrow, unlit passage. Strangely, after climbing in the dark for what seemed like several hours but could not have been more than ten minutes, I began to feel like we were descending instead of climbing. Several times I had to stop and clear my ears as if I were scuba diving. Feeling nauseous and dizzy, I wanted to sit down and rest for a while, but I could hear Fra Umberto's heavy breathing close behind me, and I was ashamed to admit that I had tired before him.

After several more minutes I couldn't help myself; my knees felt like jello and my face was burning. I didn't want to get sick. I'd read about kids who had died, choking on chunder in their headgear.

I reached for the water bottle under my chair. It's always strange, using your real hands when you're in virtual reality. With practice, I've gotten good at it, but it's still disconcerting, like seeing someone in the wrong place—a teacher at McDonald's or a lunch lady at a shoe store.

The water tasted great. It was still cold. When Fra Umberto, who hadn't heard me stop, bumped into me, I thought I was going to spill it. But nothing happened.

"Are you tired?" he asked, huffing and wheezing.

"Dizzy," I said.

"I could use a drink," he said.

When I offered him some water, he laughed.

"Where do you think I am?" he said.

I thought for a while, and then I didn't say anything.

"For all you know, I'm sitting at a terminal in Milwaukee. I have straw threaded into my headgear, and I'm drinking beer."

"I didn't think you were a player."

He clapped his hands. "Ah," he exclaimed. "You're right. Then my thirst is just a design flaw—a form of torture. I can desire, but I cannot drink. An ocean of virtual wine cannot quench my thirst."

"I'm sorry," I said.

"Don't worry," he said, patting me on the knee. "The beauty of virtual suffering is that one eventually adjusts to it. Thirst is a condition of my existence, so I learn to live with thirst."

"Where are we going?" I said after taking another sip of water.

"Up."

"Sometimes it doesn't feel like it."

"You're right," he said. "We're not going up."

"Well then, where?"

"It's neither up nor down. It's neither towards nor away."

"I don't get it."

"All movement is an illusion."

"So we could just sit here."

"Not if you want to find your friend."

"So we have to keep going."

"We're almost there."

CHAPTER SIX

Suddenly I was in a giant room filled with people, noise, and smoke all the way up to the vaulted ceiling. Fra Umberto was nowhere to be seen. The decor was gaudy: plush red carpets on the floors, Ming vases stuffed with exotic arrangements of flowers, marble columns, crystal chandeliers suspended from the vaults, giant television screens on the walls showing every sport imaginable, announcers' voices blaring a ragged cacophony, waitresses in halter-tops and mini-skirts scurrying between tables where dead-serious men in suits and women in crinolines played craps or blackjack or other indecipherable games.

Walking on tiptoe, trying to peek between two rows of shimmering slot machines, I bumped into this purple-haired lady wearing a white sequined dress two sizes too small for her. She squinted at me through Jackie Onassis glasses then grabbed me by the ear.

"Sweetheart," she muttered. "Where the hell you been? You were startin' to give me *agita*." Then she handed me a giant-size plastic cup filled with quarters. "Camman, hold onto my tokens."

She held a drink and a cigarette in her left hand. With her right, she reached into the cup, pulled out a quarter and deposited it in the slot machine in front her. She pushed a button, and cherries, horseshoes, oranges whirred.

"Would you look at this?" She waved the drink and cigarette in front of my face. "Seven ice cubes."

I recognized her nose—the Caccianemica ski slope. Now I knew who she was: my father's cousin, Auntie May. When we lived in my father's hometown, Worcester, Massachusetts, we used to visit Auntie May on Sundays after mass. She lived in a little apartment with her mother. Everybody whispered about a tragic disappointment that had left her without a husband, but they never told me anything. I was supposed to feel sorry for her, but I didn't.

I dreaded those Sunday afternoon visits. Auntie May would meet me at the door and kiss me on the lips. All afternoon, I'd feel sick to my stomach. Once, just to give her a shock, I stuck my tongue into her mouth. I thought she would scream or slap me, but instead she bit my tongue.

When I said I was going to tell my mother, she laughed at me.

"Go ahead, you little lesbian," she said. "Tell your mother you tried to French-kiss your auntie."

I couldn't imagine how she'd gotten to Dløn. I didn't think I'd scanned her.

"My name is Leo," I told her for the hundredth time.

"Sweetheart," she said, and she winked at me. "Seven ice cubes." Then she grabbed another quarter from the cup.

Her movements were strange and choppy. She didn't look entirely real. It was as if she'd been put together in chunks— as if someone had stuffed meat into her dress, and the cloth was the only thing keeping her from falling apart. The little hook at the back of her dress was broken, and the zipper had slid down a few centimeters. I was trying to think of a way to warn her without sounding rude, when she asked me a question in a strangely tender voice.

"Sweetheart," she said. "What are you doing here?"

"I'm looking for a boy," I answered.

"I thought I was your true love." Auntie May coughed. She leaned over the slot machine, and her zipper slid down another couple of notches.

I looked at the floor, ashamed.

"Who's this boy you're looking for?" she said when she'd recovered enough to speak.

"A friend. Bri's his name."

"That's not a boy. That's a cheese."

"That's his name. It's Danish, short for Brian."

"It's a good name for a dog. But I'd never call my son *brie.*"

"Have you seen him?"

"No," she muttered. "They don't allow children in here."

"I'm here."

"They saw you come in with that priest."

"Do you know Fra Umberto?"

"I don't know him. I've never seen him before. But those priests are always up to something. If you ask me, he's just another crook."

"What do you mean?"

"I don't trust any of them." She slid another quarter into the machine. "It's all a big game."

"What sort of game?"

"You ask too many questions."

If she didn't want to talk about it, I wondered why she'd brought it up. I decided to change the subject. "So you didn't see a boy, about five foot three, brown eyes, hair that's brown at the roots and blond at the tips?"

"No," Auntie May mumbled, pulling the handle on the slot machine. "I told you. They don't let children in here."

"Where do you think I should look for him?"

"Do I look like some kind of oracle? Look wherever you want." The slot machine was showing the same combination it had shown every time: a horseshoe, an orange, a bar, and cherries.

"Does it always come out the same?" I asked.

Auntie May narrowed her eyes, puffed her cigarette, and sipped her drink. Then she leaned over and whispered hot and stinky in my ear. "Can you help me fix my dress, sweetheart? I should've never worn the damned thing."

Under the dress, Auntie May's flesh was glistening with sweat. The thought of touching her made me feel sick. My first attempt was a failure; the zipper snagged, and I was afraid that I might break it.

"Use both hands," Auntie May grunted. "Put some heart into it."

I put the cup of quarters down on the floor, and like a surgeon sewing up a wound, I squeezed the two sides of Auntie May's zipper track with my left hand before dragging the handle into place with my right and locking it at the top.

Auntie May was bending over to pick up her quarters when a siren sounded in a distant corner of the room. Suddenly, all the gamblers stopped what they were doing and began to run in that direction. Auntie May dropped her drink and joined the surging crowd, shoving people out of her way, burning them with her cigarette as she ran. Now it became a stampede. Everyone was running, even the waitresses. When people fell on the ground, the others just stomped right over them.

The siren stopped as quickly as it started, but it was soon replaced by a high-pitched whistle sounding in another corner. Like a flock of sparrows blown by the wind, the whole crowd switched direction and raced towards the whistle. I saw Auntie May in the middle of the crowd, thrashing with her arms as if she were fighting an undertow, but wearing the same glazed sad look I'd seen whenever I visited her apartment.

Then I felt a hand on my arm. I turned around and saw that it was Fra Umberto.

"This sucks!" I shouted. "What's wrong with them?"

"They're having fun," he said.

"How did my aunt get here? What kind of game is this?"

Fra Umberto put his arm around my shoulder. "This is no game," he said. "You're in the mouth of the wolf. *Coraggio!* No one ever said it would be easy." Gently he steered me away from the crowd and whispered in my ear, "Come on. I'll show you something that you'll like better."

CHAPTER SEVEN

leo@fergusrules.com

We walked out a sliding door through a gallery to a balcony overlooking an open octagonal atrium. Leaning on the railing, I could see that we were inside a gigantic structure like a parking garage or shopping mall, with a domed ceiling and many floors below us. I counted eight, but there might have been more. Like the spokes of a wheel, four galleries, including the one we'd come from, extended at right angles from the atrium. Above us, the air seemed to glow with a strange silvery color, as if it was raining. Below us was a dark fiery red pit, out of which rose noxious clouds of gas and occasional hisses and moans like the sounds of an old steam furnace. As we watched, everything seemed to bend and then flip, so that what had been above us before was now below us. I felt the same queasy anxiety that I'd felt on the spiral staircase. The floors and cantilevers supporting them began to fragment and change form, coalescing into new shapes, like crystals growing or fractals unfolding. The floor no longer felt solid, but rocked and churned as if it was filled with water. Inside the atrium, strange shapes were flying through the air, obeying no observable rules of motion, some floating slowly upwards, others plummeting and disappearing in the drizzle. As I watched, I began to recognize the shapes: they were letters of the alphabet, or rather letters of many alphabets. I felt as if I had fallen into someone's screen saver or a giant bowl of soup. I tried to see if the letters would connect and form words, but they remained separate and indecipherable, like monuments, Harappan seals, or the ornate characters of illuminated manuscripts.

"A strange feat of architecture," Fra Umberto mumbled. "One must question the designer's intentions."

I would have questioned Fra Umberto's intentions had I not felt so entirely at his mercy. I wondered if he'd had anything to do with the architecture.

"Where do we go now?" I asked. "Do you have any idea where Bri is?"

"I've spoken with several characters."

"And what did they say?"

"They suggested that we visit a museum."

"A museum?"

"Yes." Fra Umberto began to walk towards a ramp that seemed to descend into the misty gray area that had previously hovered above us. "There is a most remarkable museum on the next floor down—a wax museum dedicated entirely to virtuous heathen, or, if you prefer, virtual heathen."

The ramp was crowded with little stores and stalls that seemed to be selling food, clothing, toys, jewelry, electronic gadgets, baseball cards, and other junk. I didn't see anyone shopping, just an occasional glum salesperson peering at us from behind a pile of goods. When we reached the next floor, Fra Umberto continued into the gallery directly opposite the one we'd come from without even pausing to see if I'd followed. The museum was at the end of a long row of foodstalls that smelled of sizzling pork, fried chicken, onions, garlic, and lemon grass. I called out to Fra Umberto, trying to get him to stop and sample some of the treats, but he was obsessed with the museum.

The museum had the feeling of a place that had long been forgotten. It was dusty and poorly lighted. There was no ticket booth or anything; you just walked in and started browsing. The exhibit consisted of a series of glass cases arranged along several narrow corridors. Inside each case, posed in unnatural positions, were the grotesque wax figures of heroes from the Old Testament, Ancient Chinese, Sumerian, Egyptian, Greek, and Roman philosophers, theologians, and statesmen. As we ambled by the cases, a voice that sounded like it had been recorded under water announced the date-of-birth, date-of-death, biographical highlights, and the impact each figure had on history. I love philosophy, but this was like watching one of those CDs teachers use when they can't think of anything else to do. After ten minutes, I thought I was going to fall asleep standing up.

The effect on Fra Umberto was something else entirely. He couldn't seem to decide whether to be angry, puzzled, or intrigued. He kept grunting phrases in Italian under his breath and making gestures at the cases, as if to say, "You can't be serious." He was starting to work up a good froth when we came to a case in which for the first time I recognized most of the occupants.

The case contained a group of bearded Chinese men wearing long robes. Someone had made a halfhearted attempt at decorating the case: the floor in front of the four men was painted blue to suggest a stream, and one of the philosophers held a pole with a string attached to the end. Behind them were plants vaguely suggesting bamboo that rattled awkwardly in a false wind. In virtual environments they always screw up the wind.

"So they've got the Chinese," Fra Umberto muttered.

I recognized Confucius, wearing a dark robe and playing the lyre. Him, I knew all about. In Taipei, we'd studied the Analects and learned about heroic children who passed the biggest dumplings to their fathers or took jobs after school to help pay the rent. When our teacher asked what we'd done to show filial piety, I couldn't think of anything, so I lied. When my grandmother came to visit, I told the class, I slept on the floor in the hall so she could have a room to herself. The truth was that my parents never invited her to visit us in Taipei, but I would have been happy to sleep in the street for her sake. While I'm a miserable brat to my parents, I try to respect my lola.

Fra Umberto took hold of my hand and whispered as if he feared that someone might overhear him: "If you wish to know how to lead a good life, you must read the Chinese.

"Now, the two sitting by the river with the jug of wine between them are my personal favorites—the Taoists Lao Tzu and Chuang Tzu," he continued, in his usual annoyingly loud voice. "A Taoist seeks to follow the way of nature. I won't try to explain what that means because I'm not sure that I understand. Instead, I'll just tell you a story that Chuang Tzu once told me in Apeiron where he was a pretty lively guy.

"One day, when Chuang Tzu was fishing, two officials came from the court to inform him that he'd been appointed Prime Minister.

"Chuang Tzu said to the officials, 'I've heard that there is a three-thousand-year-old tortoise shell kept on an altar in a shrine in the capital. Now tell me, if you were a turtle, would you prefer to sacrifice yourself so that you might be worshipped by some cult three thousand years from now, or would you prefer to live on dragging your tail in the mud?'

"The officials replied that the turtle would do better to go on living. At which point Chuang Tzu told the officials to go home. 'Let me stay here,' he said, 'and drag my tail in the mud.'"

Fra Umberto sighed and stroked his beard. "Temperamentally, I am more suited to Taoism than I am to Catholic monasticism. I never asked to run a monastery, or a virtual environment for that matter. I was just placed in that role. Given a choice, I would like to live by a stream, to drink rough wine and write poems. I would love to play a lyre and observe the mating habits of the whooping crane. That would be my *tao*." He laughed. "Of course nothing could be more absurd. How would I go about following the way of nature when I do not exist in nature, when I am merely a collection of information, an idea at best? How can I contemplate leading a good life when I don't have a life? Look at what they've done to poor Chuang Tzu."

Now Fra Umberto became sullen. He did not even pause as we passed a case that reminded me of a junk shop in Taipei's Snake Alley, with its display of thousands of Buddhas in all sizes and colors, including a great, green, laughing Buddha the size of a truck. Unnerved by the luminous green skin and the huge empty eyes that seemed to watch me, I rushed after Fra Umberto. I was starting to feel sorry for him until we got to the Greeks, and suddenly he became so excited I thought he was going to wet his habit.

"Ah, here are the Greeks," he grunted, ambling up to a case where two dozen dummies in robes were seated around a table so that they all faced us, like the Apostles in paintings of the Last Supper. "Some of the Greeks were just as worldly as the Chinese, but on the whole they were more concerned with questions of metaphysics: Does God exist? Do we have immortal souls? Do we have free will?"

Fra Umberto, who by now was no longer angry but merely melancholy, pointed out two of his favorite Greeks. First there was Zeno. "Through his paradoxes," Fra Umberto said, "this very clever fellow proved that motion is impossible. If a tortoise gets a head start, the great Achilles will never catch him no matter how fast he runs, for each time he covers half the distance to the tortoise, the tortoise will have moved again."

Zeno was grinning, showing off thick waxy chompers, as if he were deeply amused by being cast in wax and hence unable to move himself. I thought I understood the paradox fairly well. For the last few hours, I'd felt like I was going somewhere, but if I took off my headgear I would find that it had all been an illusion. I was still in my room.

The other Greek Fra Umberto chose to tell me about was Aristotle—a pathetic figure with a moldy complexion and half the features of his face melted away, sitting so far behind the other philosophers that he would not have been able to reach the food if there had been any on the table. Fra Umberto sighed and put his arm around my shoulder. "From my earliest childhood," he said, "I have always loved wax museums."

Was he testing me? Was it a joke? Or was he really some lunatic sitting in Milwaukee, sipping beer through a straw and leading me on this stupid journey?

"I didn't think you had a boyhood," I said.

"You're right," he mumbled sadly. "I didn't." But then he seemed to perk up again. "But I've been equipped with the memory of a most magnificent boyhood, filled with visits to museums and expositions and outings to the forest to collect insects and butterflies and late nights spent studying the works of this man by candlelight. My only problem with Aristotle is his belief that all knowledge is acquired through the senses. I have sense but no senses."

Fra Umberto was wondering aloud where the poets were housed, reciting names as if to conjure them—"Homer, Sappho, Horace, Ovid, Lucan, Li Po, Tu Fu, Vergil, Catullus" —when we turned a corner and collided with a squat little man in a torn tunic dragging a wax figure across the floor.

On closer examination, I realized that the man dragging the statue was made of wax himself. In fact, he was a magnificent sculpture, the most convincing of them all. Not that he looked human; he looked like a wax figure that was alive. Potbellied, bug-eyed, with a bulbous nose like a drunkard, he was at the same time frightening and fascinating. I had a sudden urge to ask him what wax people eat, but then Fra Umberto spoke before I could formulate my question.

"Socrates," my guide said, addressing the potbellied man. "What are you doing with John?"

I looked closely. The dummy being dragged across the floor was John Lennon. His face was unformed. It looked like a line drawing, like one of Lennon's self-portraits.

"I'm taking him to the stewpot," the wax man mumbled, sliding his hands into John's armpits and balancing him against his hip.

"What do you mean the stewpot?"

"We have a shortage of candles."

"So you're melting down John?"

"I'm melting down all of the poets."

My guide hissed under his breath.

"Do you like our museum?" Socrates said, as if he hadn't heard a thing.

"Don't be ridiculous," Fra Umberto finally growled, ignoring his question. "Why are you melting the poets?"

Socrates rolled his eyes. "The museum is an educational institution," he said. "We wouldn't want the young people who visit us to be misled, would we?"

"You feel that poets mislead the youth?"

"Poetry with all of its wailing and whining makes the youth softheaded and weak. How can we hope to defend our city if the youth are subject to the softening of poetry?"

There was something bombastic and repellent now about the old man. You could see how thickly the wax had been piled on him.

It was clear that their argument wasn't getting anywhere. I was impatient. I had heard this spiel before in Dr. Jack's class. The whole class had gotten into an argument. The anti-poets had won, and even then I had barely listened. But Fra Umberto, his small eyes dancing, looked ready to pick a fight. It seemed that Fra Umberto had forgotten what we were doing in Dløn.

"We're looking for someone," I blurted. "Maybe you can help us to find him."

"I see," Socrates said, letting John slide back onto the floor.

He fell with a pathetic whine, like a toy car running out of spin. I couldn't help but look at John, whose music used to sustain me in the days before my stepfather had given me my first computer. John's left cheek was deformed now, a straight line against the floor.

Socrates continued, "Are you certain that he wants to be found?"

"You can't get away with it," Fra Umberto interrupted, trying to pull John away. Instinctively, I moved to help the monk, to save John from entirely decomposing.

Socrates rolled his eyes again, smiled condescendingly, and gave Fra Umberto a push that sent him sprawling. Holding onto Fra Umberto's robe, I fell with him, landing against a solid, rather gelatinous thigh. "Would you like to talk in my office?" Socrates challenged.

Fra Umberto got up. I lay groggy on the floor. The monk had seemed on the verge of losing his cool, but then he threw up his hands in a gesture of surrender. "Why not?"

We left John, the way builders might leave a piece of wood or a length of pipe. Wistfully, I looked back at him. It was sad that in Dløn, he was only a thing of wax.

As we followed the old man down a long, dimly lit corridor, Fra Umberto took hold of my shoulder and whispered something in my ear. "Don't sit too close to him," he warned.

"What his questions do to your mind, his hands will try to do to your body."

"He only likes boys," I retorted.

"Don't be too sure," he chuckled. "Besides, by the look of you, who's to know?"

The office was reminiscent of the glass cases that contained the other wax figures. It was empty except for a table, three gray metal folding chairs, and a filing cabinet in the corner. Socrates sat down and gestured for us to do the same. I chose the seat farthest from him.

"The first question you must ask yourself is why you are searching for this person," he said, stroking his beard. "What is your motivation?" I marveled at the sight of him. Although he was made of wax, Socrates's gestures and voice were utterly convincing.

"I want to help him," I said.

"And how would you define *help*?" he said.

"You know, help," I said, suddenly feeling confused. "I mean, if he's in trouble."

"If he is in trouble..." Socrates nodded. "Now, that is an interesting point. How should we define *trouble*? Was Odysseus in trouble when he called upon Athena to help him overcome his wife's suitors? If so, why did he disguise himself from Athena when she came to him?"

I looked at Fra Umberto. He was bent over his glasses, polishing them again with maniacal intensity. The room felt hot and stuffy as if it had been sealed for centuries.

"I see that you are referring to the work of a poet," Fra Umberto said maliciously.

Socrates looked at him as if he were pained. "Because I choose to eject poets from my sphere does not mean I do not admire them," he said with complete contempt.

Fra Umberto looked properly humbled.

"I'm not sure I understand," I interrupted, trying to get back to the point. "I am only looking for a boy."

"Ah yes," said the philosopher. "Let me put it another way. You might be conducting your search simply because you wish to gain something in exchange. Your affection may be an affection of the senses and nothing more. Or, on the contrary, you may be searching for virtuous reasons. To be moved from within is soulful. To be moved from without is soulless. If you are moved from within, you may be genuinely concerned, in an ideal sense, for the well-being of this person."

"Yes," I said, trying to avoid his question. I didn't know whether I was moved from within or without. I liked Bri. I liked the way he looked, but mostly I liked his sense of humor. I liked the way he had gotten me back for making fun of him in class. The next day, he had e-mailed me this message: "My revenge is friendship. Try as you will, you'll never get rid of me."

"Let us assume that your intentions are good." Socrates nodded and went on tugging at his beard, which looked like it might pop loose from the wax of his chin at any moment. "You must look upon the face of your beloved and reverence him. And if you are not afraid of being thought a madman you must sacrifice to him as to an image of a god. Then, as you gaze at him, you will feel a sudden warmth. This is your wings unfolding. It will feel something like your gums felt when you were cutting teeth—sort of itchy and effervescent."

"How can I look upon his face if I don't know where he is," I protested.

"Well, that is a problem," Socrates mumbled, still tugging at his beard. "My suggestion is that you take up the study of mathematics."

"Mathematics," I said.

The philosopher smiled. "Would you like to see some slides?" he asked, as if to indicate that he was through discussing Bri.

Fra Umberto laughed. "Of course," he said.

"Good," said the philosopher, and he turned out the light. After a moment, I heard the sound of a fan, and a little block of light appeared on the wall in front of us. But instead of showing us slides, Socrates began to make shadow puppets on the wall. First he made a rabbit with long floppy ears. "Now don't turn around," he said. "Guess what this one is."

"A cat?" I said.

"Indeed," Socrates mumbled, his voice edged with disappointment.

"Show us the slides, show us the slides," Fra Umberto cackled.

Now Socrates made a wolf—much more clearly than any I'd ever seen before, with sharp fangs and fur on its ears. "What if I were to tell you that I don't have any slides?" he said.

"I'd say you were cracked," Fra Umberto said.

"I don't know how you can persist in being a materialist when you have no material substance whatsoever," Socrates grunted. His voice sounded different—less dignified, more high-pitched and nervous. I turned around to look at him, and sure enough he was morphing. As I watched him, he grew taller, more imposing. His beard turned brown, his eyes yellow. His old ragged robe was replaced by a flawless, freshly pressed white toga. "Like myself, you exist purely as a function of electronic memory."

Now the wolf, scraping and panting, began to detach itself from the screen. I could smell the dead meat stench of its breath. Just when I was sure that it was going to leap at us,

Fra Umberto swung around and knocked the projector onto the floor.

"You're not Socrates! You're not Plato!" Fra Umberto shouted. "You're not a philosopher of any sort. You're a tyrant made of wax." Then he took me by the arm and led me out of the door, shouting as we ran: "I'd rather drag my tail in the mud than lord it over all exhausted shades!"

CHAPTER EIGHT

Although I would swear that we left the museum through the same door that we entered, we emerged from it in a different place entirely. It felt as if we were outside, in a narrow and crowded back street of an old European or Asian city— Malate, Bangkok, or Genoa, I couldn't tell which. The air was thick with the smell of burned fat, ginger, soy sauce, garlic, and the body odors of people and animals. There was no sidewalk, and the street was badly paved. Fra Umberto had to hoist up his habit to keep it from getting caught on the loose stones or soaked in the puddles that had accumulated in the holes that riddled the street.

Right away, we were caught in the current of people, all rushing in the same direction. Oddly, there were no women or children in the crowd, only men. Some of them were dressed like businessmen, with coats and ties; some wore jeans, and others were nearly naked. They weren't speaking to each other, but all the same, they created a terrible din. Belching, gibbering, and grunting, they nudged and shoved each other like kids in a lunch line. Even more disgusting was the way they kept scratching themselves and picking at their armpits and crotches as if they had chicken pox or scabies.

Maybe because I was afraid of falling and getting trampled, it took me a while to notice our surroundings. The shops were small and decrepit, but their displays were lit with lurid pink, yellow, and blue neon lights. I assumed they were just selling food, trinkets, and other junk. But after a while, as I looked more closely, I noticed that each window contained a freak show, each more bizarre and sickening than the previous one. There were girls with beaks and eagles' talons and feathers growing from their skin. There were boys sprouting leaves and bark, with vines and epiphytes extending from their armpits. One display featured a kick-line of morphs stranded halfway between girl- and goathood, dressed in high heels and bikinis, and spinning round and round on a Chinese service table. I saw a boy whose skin was transparent: you could see his heart throbbing away. It reminded of the time we'd cut open an anesthetized frog in science class.

After a while, I noticed another weird feature of this street. If I became interested in a particular window-show, the traffic seemed to slow down. In fact, as I became more absorbed, the people around me slowed to a standstill, and I could easily slip around them, over to the window that interested me. But if something distracted me and my attention wandered for a moment, I would find myself back in the crowd being tossed forward like a twig in a stream.

Once I stopped before a window where morphs were hanging from hooks, like pieces of meat in a butcher's shop. I could not take my eyes off a cow with a boy's face and hair: a real cow/boy. He looked at me in a way that made me feel sick and helpless. When Fra Umberto tried to cover my eyes with the sleeve of his habit, I bit his finger. It was hairy and hard like a stick of wood, and I almost gagged. He let me go, but it was too late. We slid back into the stream of itchy, stinking men.

At that moment, I decided to get rid of Fra Umberto. So far, he had caused me nothing but grief and aggravation. Scooting between legs and around sagging bellies, I lost him in the crowd. Once I was sure we were separated, I stopped at a window displaying mermaids. They were kept in tanks illuminated by hideous pink, orange, and green gas bubbles.

Their hair glittered with tacky neon highlights, and they had big, sad, unblinking fish eyes. Their tails were long and scaly. Under other circumstances, this would not have disturbed me. Traveling in Apeiron, I had seen mermaids by the hundreds, but it had always been a glimpse—a splash and a shimmer that left me questioning my senses. Here, in the tanks, the tails seemed like torture devices. There was no room for the mermaids to swim or even to straighten themselves, so they rested their full weight on tails bent awkwardly to the side, their flesh pressed like packaged ham against the walls of their tanks. Every few minutes one of them would stir up a storm of smoky bubbles, only to shift her tail into a new and equally awkward position.

One of the mermaids was about my age. I tried waving and knocking on the glass of her tank. But she did not look at me. Her eyes seemed to be focused on the walls of the tank or maybe they were just open and not focused at all. Looking at her made me feel guilty—as if I was somehow to blame. I knew if Fra Umberto had been there, he would have told me not to worry. "She's only a character," he would have said. "She doesn't really feel anything."

After a while, I went crazy and started punching and kicking the tank. But it was like fighting against bread dough. My hand sank into a warm spongy substance, and when I pulled it out there was no way to see that it had ever been there. I tried putting my hand in slowly, and soon it was buried to the wrist, the elbow, the shoulder. I would have stuck my head in too if I hadn't been interrupted by a tap on the shoulder.

Turning around I saw a short bald man in a yellow t-shirt with thick red hair growing out of his ears and nostrils. He was barely an inch taller than me, but he leaned back on his heels so that he could look down at me while he muttered:

"Gawking Arabs, gawking Dane,
Gawking painter in the rain,
Gawking Frenchmen, gawking Jews,
Gawking Poles in tennis shoes.
Gawking Blacks, gawking Whites,
Gawking Swedes with overbites,
Gawking Germans, gawking Swiss,
Gawking priest in state of bliss,
Gawking morning, gawking night,
Gawking whether wrong or right,
Gawking yellow, gawking red,
Gawking screwy acid head,
Gawking teeth, gawking jaws,
Gawking in your underdrawers."

When he was finished, he scratched himself some more, picked his nose, and smiled. "So, you likes the fishy?" he gurgled, his throat thick with mucus.

I was too surprised to answer. His skin was splotchy like an old banana's.

"You want to get inside with fishy?" He continued, and I caught a whiff of his breath—a mixture of old socks and *bagoong,* the sickening shrimp fry my lola makes every Saturday morning.

I do not know where Fra Umberto had been while I was watching the mermaid, but he came to my rescue now like a Saturday morning superhero. After elbowing the little man into the putty glass of the mermaid tank, he put his arm around my shoulder and led me back into the crowded street.

"Are you really a priest?" I asked him.

"I'm supposed to be a Dominican monk," he said. "That was the order of Saint Thomas Aquinas, who brought reason and faith together. Of course, in the Middle Ages, the Dominicans were also responsible for all sorts of monstrosities, burning people at the stake and so on."

"What about you?"

"As you know, I'm not even a person," he said, sounding miserable.

"What happens to those children?" I asked.

"It's best not to think about it."

"Why are you patronizing me?"

"Don't be quick to judge what you've just seen," he said. "The morphs are the creatures of other people's desires. It is not their choice to be on display, nor was it my choice that you should see them."

"What about the men?"

"Their desires will keep them shuffling and scratching by the displays. Have you ever seen a Mobius strip?"

"Of course," I said.

"Well, this road is designed like a Mobius strip: it turns back on itself for all eternity. We've already gone around once. Two more times and we'd be like them—incapable of breaking the cycle. But now we need to pay attention. There's a crack in a wall of a building up ahead. If we jump through it, we'll get back to the atrium. Make sure you close your eyes before we hit the wall; you might not make it through if you don't." And with that, he steered me straight at a wall that looked as solid as any I'd ever seen.

I closed my eyes at the last moment, not because he'd told me to, but because I was afraid to see what was going to happen. When I opened them, I saw my legs sliding through a crack no wider than a paper cut, and for a moment I glimpsed the stinking crowd of men looking like cartoon figures going round and round on a twisted piece of celluloid.

CHAPTER NINE

Suddenly we were once again standing at a railing overlooking the atrium. Up and down, clockwise and counter shapes were still churning, still changing places; the walls, ceiling, and floor remained indefinite; and occasionally a weightless letter or symbol would float by, but somehow this no longer bothered me. It was as if my mind had adjusted. But my feet were aching, and the smells from the food stands were driving me crazy.

"I'm starving," I said once I'd caught my breath. "Can't we get something to eat?"

"The fact is that I'm not particularly interested in dragging my tail in the mud," Fra Umberto said, as if to change the subject. "What I would love to do, if only for a few hours, is to become material so that I might cook a meal and eat it. Any meal would do, no matter how humble: a dish of polenta and gravy, a plate of spaghetti alla putanesca. The wine could be rough and simple—a Friuli table wine or a cheap Chianti." Then he grunted and patted his stomach. "Whatever you do, don't buy anything here. Don't eat anything. Don't try on any clothes."

"Don't tell me," I said. "If I buy anything, I'll never get out."

"That's right."

"You sound like my lola."

"Who's your lola?"

"My grandmother. My mother's mother. I live with her."

"And what does she know about Dløn?"

"Nothing. But she knows all about demons and magic and angels and little people."

"Well, make sure you follow your lola's advice while you're in Dløn."

"Isn't this getting kind of corny? I mean, do you get paid for this? Is there going to be some killer charge on my father's account? How much is one hour online to Dløn worth?"

Fra Umberto chuckled. "You still think you're playing a game. Well, then go ahead. Go shopping." He stepped aside and pointed towards a row of shops with stylish window displays. I was reminded of my mother's favorite dives: Macy's in New York, Copley Plaza in Boston, or Shangri La in Manila— everything was steel and glass: bright, clean, and dazzling. "Only two hundred and forty-one shopping days left until Christmas. Hurry up. Maybe you'll find something nice for Bri."

I was sick of him. One of the great things about games is that they give you control. They don't force you to follow some mysterious agenda that keeps changing according to the moods of your parents or teachers. Every game has a set of rules, and once you master those rules you can win. In Dløn there was no sense to anything. I was relying on Fra Umberto to help me find Bri, who either was or wasn't in Dløn. Nothing that had happened so far seemed to be getting us any closer to that goal. Fra Umberto just seemed to be winging it—as if he didn't care whether or not we found Bri, or as if he was using the search as an excuse to suck me into some scheme of his own.

I decided I would call his bluff. I went shopping. I raced up the down escalator, and I messed around with fishing poles, golf clubs, an electric piano, a remote control car. I put the tag from a girdle on a refrigerator. I played a video game I'd never seen before, and I watched a wall of televisions all with different shows on. The only problem was that I didn't have any money, and none of the shopkeepers were willing to let me use my father's account number. I was about to steal a croissant from the display outside a fancy French restaurant when someone tugged at my shirt.

It was Marco from my Humanities class. With his Angels cap pulled down over his eyes and this diabolical smile on his face, he looked like himself—only bigger. I knew that in real life he was smaller than me, because he was the only boy in our class who was, but now, though he was still a hair shorter than me, he was about fifty pounds heavier.

"Pare, what are you doing here?" he said, speaking Taglish, a mixture of Filipino and English. "Are you hungry?"

"Talaga," I answered in Filipino. "Starving."

He reached into his pocket and pulled out a fistful of dried squid. It looked stringy and tough as shoe leather. "This is the best, *pare.* No matter how much you eat, you don't get any fuller. You can just keep on eating." Although his cheeks were full, he kept stuffing more and more squid into his mouth. As he chewed, a stream of brown saliva dribbled from his lips onto his chin, and he seemed to swell, to grow bigger right before my eyes. After swallowing a mouthful, he reached into his pocket for more. Soon, he was twice my size.

"You're getting really big, *pare,"* I said, trying to act nonchalant.

"It's nothing," he said, and he held the bag out to me. "You should try some."

"That's all right," I said. "I ate already."

He shoveled some more squid into his mouth and spoke before he was finished chewing, so little flecks of tentacle and squid juice came flying out of his mouth. "So, what are you doing here, *pare?"*

The stench of his breath was almost unbearable. "I'm looking for Bri," I said, edging away from him.

"That weird guy in Humanities class? What do you want with him?"

"He's not weird."

"Touchy, touchy. You're not, you know, in love or something, are you?"

"No," I said.

"I hope not. Because, *pare,* I don't think he'll ever fall in love with you after what happened in Humanities class." He chuckled. "Who Goes with Fairgoose?"

"That's not funny."

"It's your joke, *pare.*"

"And I say it's not funny."

"Okay," he said, and he held out a fistful of squid as a peace offering.

"I don't want any," I said, brushing it away. "Have you seen Bri?"

Marco chewed pensively for a while before answering: "Not down here. But I'll help you look for him."

"Do you know your way around?"

"Sure," he said.

But when he tried to move, he couldn't. Each time he stood up, he just rolled over like a giant egg.

"You'd better cut down on the squid, *pare,*" I said.

"I can't," he said. "The more I eat, the more I want to eat. And this bag never runs out."

"Where would you look for Bri?" I said.

With what remained of his chin, he nodded at a hallway that went off to the left. For a while I felt bad for him, but then I got away fast. I didn't want to be around when he exploded.

I entered the first store I saw and ran into a group of girls from my old school in Walnut, California. Amanda,

Lara, Soo Jin, and Gihani were all mall-rats, fashion-phreaks, like-girls extraordinaire. As far as I could remember, the only thing that exceeded my hatred for them was their disdain for me. But, as I was learning, everything in Dløn is screwy .

"Look," said Amanda. "It's, like, Leo."

"Cool," said Lara, batting her eyes. "I didn't know you were, like, into shopping."

"We should, you know—dress her up or something," Soo Jin giggled. "I mean, are those, like, Wranglers she's wearing?"

"And look at the *boots,*" Lara screeched.

"I like my clothes," I mumbled.

"What?" Gihani said, squinting so her nose and forehead got all wrinkled like a bulldog's. "Are you, like, going mountain climbing?"

Amanda took me by the shoulder and spun me around. "I'm so bored," she said.

"I know," Lara giggled. "Let's, like, spend some money."

The cadence of their speech coupled with the intonation of their voices had a numbing effect. Listening to them, I lost the ability to think for myself. Before I knew what had happened, I was following them from shop to shop like a stunned fish, letting them dress me in baseball caps, fedoras, bandanas, wigs, and sunglasses in different colors, sports coats five sizes too big for me, colognes that made me stink like my stepfather going out on a date with a girlfriend, argyle socks, silk ascots, flannel boxer shorts, jeans that were too tight in the crotch, or jeans that sagged to my knees, neckties, rings, bracelets, watches with pictures of cartoon characters on them, eyeglasses, belts, suspenders, earrings, platform sneakers, a nose ring. Amanda wanted me to pierce my nipple so I could wear a ring there. Lara suggested my navel.

When at last they had me outfitted the way they liked, in high-top Reeboks, Pierre Cardin socks, Levis—loose but not baggy—a fifty-five dollar white t-shirt designed by some famous Italian, Ray-Bans, a nose ring but none in the nipple or navel, they started fighting about my hair. Soo Jin thought they should cut it all off except for my bangs. Gihani and Amanda wanted to grease it back like Dylan's on 90210. But Lara said that was corny.

"It should just be messy. Did you see *Reality Bites*? I cried when Ethan Hawke came back to Winona Ryder. I mean, if only Leo had, like, facial hair."

"Yeah, I know," Amanda said. "I have, like, a Planet of the Apes on my shoulders."

"Duh," Lara squinted and rolled her eyes so only the whites were showing. "It's, like, a planet of regrets, stupid."

"I don't know," Soo Jin said. "I think Leo would make, like, a really beautiful girl."

"Duh!" shouted Lara.

"Duh!" shouted Amanda. "Duh! Duh! Duh!"

They were hovering around me, holding scissors and combs and brushes, when suddenly they were interrupted by a sound like a sail filling up with wind. Giant winged shadows appeared on the floor, and all four girls screeched and ran down different aisles. I was too stunned to react. And what descended on me was a flock of birds like none I'd ever seen before. They had the wings of pterodactyls but the bodies of seven-foot-tall Barbie dolls, with huge molded plastic breasts jutting straight out from their chests and hair of shimmering platinum nylon. The Barbies were smiling fashion-model smiles, a gash of white paint between two red ones, and their eyes were huge and unblinking. The eyelashes had been painted on their faces in the same bright shade of blue as the eyes. Circling above me, they screeched in high-pitched voices, "Nike, Guess, Benetton, Levis! Tommy, Tommy, Tommy-boy!"

The first bird that dove at me knocked the Ray Bans off my face, smashing them on the ground. With her bright red fingernails, the next Barbie ripped a hole in my new t-shirt. But the third one, who seemed larger and more powerful than the rest, lifted me by my belt loop and flew off towards the atrium. Despite their size, these birds flew with incredible speed and grace, darting among the pillars and signs, deftly avoiding all obstacles.

I was sure that I was going to be eaten, but I was not really all that frightened. Playing virtual reality games, I'd grown accustomed to this sort of situation. I was in the clutches of an evil beast; now my task was to free myself. This was more satisfying than wandering around with a ponderous priest or having weird encounters with friends and former classmates.

At the atrium, we flew right over Fra Umberto's head. Seeing the familiar bald crown from this perspective was somehow reassuring. But instead of shaking his fist and shouting curses, he cupped his hands and shouted words of encouragement. *"Forza! Coraggio! Vi raccomando!* Always turn to the left," I heard him shout. But the rest was cryptic, blurred by the sudden rush of wind in my ears, as the giant bird dove into the pit of the atrium.

Effortlessly dodging the alphabet soup that floated in the air around us, we plummeted unrestrained for what seemed like several minutes, the rush of wind bringing tears to my eyes, my stomach dropping into my intestines, the familiar weightless giddiness tickling my crotch. I do not know why I wasn't more afraid. Maybe it was because I felt that I would finally have the chance to see if Dløn was any different from Apeiron and the other virtual environments I'd played around in. Could these giant Barbie dolls really hurt me in some way that the game-dragons could not? Might you be virtually killed and die in reality too? I didn't think so.

When the Barbie spread her wings to break our fall, we hovered as if a parachute had opened. Unlike the floors above, the level belonging to these birds was cavernous, forested with bare-branched concrete trees extending towards a high, black, vaulted ceiling. The air was thick with a familiar fetid stench, like overripe cheese or durian. Perched in the trees were hundreds, maybe thousands, of these beasts, some of them sleeping, standing up with their heads lolling onto their chests, others eating, ripping the clothes from the unfortunate creatures who had come into their clutches, tearing into the cloth with shimmering metal teeth. I laughed when I realized that it was my new outfit that had attracted the beast's attention and not the flesh inside it. I decided that I would make things easier for her by stripping the moment we landed.

No sooner had this plan taken shape in my mind than the loop by which she'd been transporting me tore and set me free. If we had not been flying so low and if she'd not been taken by surprise, I have no doubt the beast would have been able to catch me again before I landed. But that was not to be. The fall was quick and surprisingly painless. I fell into a sad, slow-moving river of some stinking white substance, filled with curds, like milk gone sour or pigeon shit. Before giving up on me, my former captor swooped at my head screeching "Tommy-boy" and dropping a fat white turd on my face.

I tried to wipe it off with the sleeve of my shirt, but it was useless. I was coated in that foul substance. I considered climbing up the banks to get out of the river, but then I decided that was a lousy plan. The banks were steep and splattered with more guano, and there were Barbies standing guard at twenty-meter intervals, staring at the river of white sludge and picking at their feathers.

Fortunately the melted-cheese consistency of the sludge in the river kept me from sinking beyond my chest. As I rode with the sluggish current, I saw dozens of lifeless bodies, floating face-down and naked, and I felt lucky to have escaped. After a while, the river flowed into a cave. I do not know how it happened—something about the darkness, the steady movement of the river, the familiar stench—but I drifted off to sleep.

CHAPTER TEN

When I woke up, I found that I was no longer floating down the river but had somehow been transported to my own room. It was not my room in Manila. Mostly, it reminded me of my room in Worcester—only there were certain differences in light and other minute, almost imperceptible details that made it seem like another place or rather a weird jumble of various places. On my desk stood a lamp I'd left in Walnut because the socket was broken, and the walls were decorated with drawings I'd done when we lived in Lima. I didn't recognize the TV at all. The whir of the central air-conditioning reminded me of Jakarta, but the huge, spongy bed and the faint smell of fried ginger were from Beijing. The mistakes were like a joke—like someone winking at me, saying, "See, it's not just that I can re-create your memories; I can add details you never expected. I can mix things up and re-combine things in ways that you never imagined."

I went to the bathroom to wash off. There was a bathtub, but no shower. I ran the water and got in with my clothes on. The water looked like water and it felt like water, but it didn't work like water. If anything, it hardened the guano on my clothing and skin so it felt like I was covered in cement. I was reminded of the early game environments in which objects could only be used in certain ways. A shoe was only good for walking. You couldn't take it off and hit a monster with it. I didn't think the designers of Dløn would make that kind of mistake. It was just another problem they were posing. It was their way of saying, things aren't always what they seem.

I left my clothes in the tub, and for a while I walked around the room naked. I have always enjoyed being naked. I have always enjoyed the way nakedness freaks other people out. Once, when I was in first grade, I took off my clothes in class to protest a worksheet that the teacher had given us. There was nothing unusual about the worksheet. It just wasn't very challenging, and I didn't feel like doing it.

For several minutes, the teacher tried to coax me into putting on my clothes. The other kids giggled, but they were afraid to say anything to me. Eventually, the teacher lost her patience and started to yell at me. I just sat there singing Christmas songs with no clothes on. Finally, my mother had to come to school and get me dressed. We never talked about it, but that was the end of my career at that school.

When I sat down on the bed to think about where I was and how I'd gotten there, I heard familiar voices through the wall. My mother and my stepfather were arguing. I wondered if it was a new argument or if they were just fighting the old one over again. But even with my ear pressed against the wall, I could only make out an occasional word. Of course, I didn't really want to hear them. Their arguments were always the same.

I lay down and put a pillow over my head, and suddenly I could hear them clearly, as if they were standing in my room.

"If only you could be a little bit responsible," my stepfather whined.

My mother countered with an angry monologue, growling and cursing in a voice thick with contempt. I heard the word "sleaze" again and again, emerging like "Mary" and "Lord" from the clutter of Lola's whispered prayers.

My stepfather countered, wheedling and coaxing in a voice like condensed milk. "You can't buy every Chinese medicine chest you see. You have to plan these things."

"Are you going to lecture me on impulses?" my mother said. "You? Don't make me laugh."

"No," he shouted. "Only on responsibility. Money doesn't grow on trees like coconuts."

My mother snorted and cursed him in Tagalog.

My stepfather was silent for a while. When he spoke, he had changed his tactics. He was using his rational tone of voice—the one designed to make you feel that you're being totally unreasonable. "You just have to take into consideration our responsibilities."

My mother became furious. "Responsiblities? You want to talk about responsibilities?" she shouted.

I'd heard that one before. The litany of his crimes would surface, a sordid string of names. There were so many—and some of the names were so common—Jill and Jan and Joan—from Bangkok, Bombay and Bolivia—that I wondered if my mom were making it up, pulling random, noncommittal epithets from a hat.

Now came a gaping silence—filled only by the whir of the air-conditioner and the chirp of a lizard in my room. I was looking for the lizard when the crescendo began. My stepfather was hurling things at the walls. There were things that crashed and shattered, others that hissed and crunched, and a few that rustled, whirred, and exploded finally like light bulbs or water balloons. It sounded as if he was playing a video game. After a brief lull, while he snorted and gasped to catch his breath, my mother was whimpering, still muttering about sleaze as if it were her mantra, her protective song.

I don't know why they got married. All they ever seemed to do was fight. I do know that I caused my parents' breakup.

I've seen pictures of my father and mother when they were first married. It seemed they were always smiling and holding onto one another. They loved to travel, and they were happy together. I know that they consider me a mistake.

How can I say for sure? Answer this simple question. What do you do with mistakes? You hide them. You send them halfway around the world so that someone else can deal with them. There is nothing worse than eating breakfast with your mistake, driving her to school, or telling her a bedtime story.

I have received five letters from my mother since I arrived in the Philippines. In them, she assures me that she and my stepfather are happy, that they are working out their differences. I couldn't care less.

Dad has not written once. I tell myself that he has gone insane or is being held captive somewhere. I was seven when my parents were divorced. I don't remember my father very well, but I know he can't be as bad as my stepfather.

Lola says that my stepfather is exactly like my father, but I think she's blind. My father looks like a sculpture by Michelangelo. He used to sing to me in Tuscan dialect. My stepfather, on the other hand, is ashamed of being Filipino. He claims that he's Spanish, and he tries to act like he's American. Sometimes, when we go to a mall or something, I'll ask him a question in Tagalog, just to puncture his all-American pretenses. The strategy always works. He gets so pissed, he can't control himself: he starts cursing me in Tagalog, right in front of all these strangers. Then I just walk away from him, acting like I don't understand.

After a while, when the argument just kept going on and on, I began to wonder if I was dreaming. It's not always easy to tell whether you're asleep or whether you're awake in virtual reality. After flying the same jet and fighting the same battles for ten or fifteen hours, you're likely to go on dreaming of flight patterns and evasion tactics and twitching your trigger finger when you sleep.

One way to tell if you're really awake is to take a pee. When I lock myself in for long trips, I always tube up. If you're asleep you might wet your pants by accident, but you can't micturate on command. Either way, the tube is protection.

Another thing that occurred to me was that maybe I was dead. Maybe I had drowned in that big white river of Barbie guano. Stupid things like that happen to kids all the time: they fall off of skateboards in front of buses or they get locked into meat freezers. I've heard about kids who died in virtual reality, but only on the gossip-net. Anyway, I imagine the test is the same. I've never heard of anyone pissing in the afterlife. If your bladder can still work, it probably means you're awake and you're alive.

If you're skeptical about that approach, I have another one: I look for reading material I've never seen before. I examine it closely, trying to discover unfamiliar details or words that I don't understand. It's not like you could sit down and start reading Immanuel Kant's *Critique of Pure Reason* in a dream. At least I couldn't.

When I looked around the room for something to read, I couldn't find anything. That was one thing the designers of Dløn hadn't bothered to imitate. And that was weird when you considered that they were the ones who'd been stealing the words from Fra Umberto's books. I wondered if they'd done this on purpose, just to make sure you couldn't figure out if you were alive or dead. I sat and thought for a while about Dløn, what it was, who controlled it, whether it was really this big conspiracy, but then I started getting antsy and cold.

I looked through the drawers in the dresser. I found all the clothes I'd ever owned. There were t-shirts, jeans, dresses, leotards with holes in the toes from gymnastics, my favorite Irish fisherman's sweater, underwear in every size up to the present. I used some kid clothes to clean the guano from my face, my hair, my hands. In places, it was stuck on like oil paint. It didn't matter what I did, I couldn't get it off. When I was satisfied that I'd done my best, I got dressed in exactly the same clothes I'd worn when I'd gone to visit the monastery, except that I put on an extra pair of socks.

After lacing my boots, I decided to turn on the TV. At least that would drown out the argument. I flicked through the channels without finding anything interesting. There was sumo wrestling, a German movie dubbed in English and subtitled in Bahasa-Indonesian, Malaysian soccer, Indian kuchipudi dancing, a Nigerian melodrama, and ads in French and Tagalog for shampoo, toothpaste, and Marlboro country.

Finally, I settled on a station that looked something like MTV Asia; only it was completely different. I found it reassuring that I had never seen any of the acts before. After a lame Thai rap act (sort of like LL Cool J without rhythm) and a bizarre Japanese ska orchestra, there was a Chinese grunge number. First the camera focused on the mosh pit. But this was no ordinary mosh pit. It was Tiananmen Square, and there were a million people all dressed like Chairman Mao moshing in front of the Forbidden City. The dancers were frantic and crazy. They were stomping on top of each other. Suddenly the camera cut to the stage. Instead of a band, there were a dozen women (or men dressed like women) holding fans and wearing the bright-colored dresses, masks, and feathers of the Beijing opera. The strangest thing was that the music that seemed to be coming from them was nothing new. It sounded more or less like Metallica, only with Mandarin lyrics. The singer just kept singing the same lyrics over and over, and after a while I realized that I knew the words. It was the Ballad of Mu-lan. I had learned it for

Chinese class in Beijing. The teacher had not liked my choice, but I had told her that I identified with Mu-lan.

Father and mother, hearing of their daughter's return,
Go outside the city walls to help and support her by the hand.
Elder sister, hearing the younger one's return,
Goes over her rouge make-up in front of the door.
Little brother, hearing elder sister's return,
Sharpens the knife, swish-swashing toward the pig and sheep.
I open the door to my eastern chamber;
I sit on the bed in my western chamber.
I slip off my wartime's robe,
And put on my old-time dress.
Facing the window, I arrange my cloud-like hair;
Looking into the mirror, I adorn myself with a yellow patch.
I go out to the door to greet my messmates,
And they are stunned with surprise:
Though they have marched with her for twelve years,
They have not known that Mu-lan is a girl.

The male rabbit has skipping-legs,
The female rabbit has bleary eyes;
The two walk side by side on the ground
And none can tell the male from the female.

After I recognized the poem, for some reason I got so depressed that I had to turn the TV off. I thought about skipping-legs, and I felt my eyes getting bleary. My friend, Qi, had written the poem for me on rice paper using ink she'd made herself. Somehow, in one of our moves, I'd lost her original painting. My only consolation was that I had scanned it into my journal. Now, I felt sick at the thought that Qi's beautiful calligraphy had been sucked into Dløn.

My parents were still arguing in the other room—my stepfather going on and on about responsibility, my mother faint from crying. On the end note of their fights, I always felt oddly, weakly sad about my mother. It was that sound of weeping—that gurgling, choked despair: I always felt I should do something, hug her, or pelt her husband with pebbles, or start dancing around to distract them. But try as I might, in Dløn, though I heard them plainly, I was as separate and distant from their quarrel as if their sounds were simply alien chronicles from MTV. I could try to reach out to my mother's whimper, but for all I knew, the forlorn sound was just background bass in a lurid Indo-European singing act.

Outside, the streetlights were glowing even though it wasn't dark yet. A figure wearing a robe sat down on a bench across the street. I recognized him almost immediately. He seemed to be looking right at me, but when I called his name and waved at him, he did not respond at all. When it started snowing, he got up and began to pace.

I decided to go to the window and jump out since I was only on the second floor. I started to walk across the room, but I soon found that I couldn't get anywhere. I would set my sights on a line on the floor, a grain in the wood or the seam between boards, but each time I reached a new mark a whole new stretch of floor would appear in front of me.

In this way, I walked and I walked until I felt exhausted, but I never got any closer to the window. It occurred to me that maybe the floor was some sort of treadmill, the kind they have in hotel gyms for traveling exercise freaks. But if that had been true, I would have slid backwards as soon as I stopped walking. Instead, nothing happened at all.

In the meantime, it had gotten dark outside and several centimeters of snow had fallen. Fra Umberto, pacing back and forth, had made a trail in front of the bench. I tried calling him again, but there was still no response. I wondered if he had seen me and was just ignoring me. Maybe that was all a part of the game.

I stopped and tried to calculate the distance to the window. It couldn't have been more than six meters. I thought that maybe I would have more success if I concentrated on walking part of the way instead of trying to walk all the way at once. If I walked halfway and then halfway again, I would eventually get to the window. With this in mind, I set out once more. But after walking for what seemed like an hour, I was beat, and I still had half the floor to cross. Anyway, when I looked up, it had stopped snowing and Fra Umberto was gone.

This made me think about Bri. Even if I could figure out where he was, I knew he would have gone some place else by the time I got there. And if I followed him to this new place, he'd have gone somewhere else again. So, unless I could find out where he was going and get there before he did, I would never be able to catch him. It seemed that Zeno had been right after all.

I turned the TV on again, partly to drown out my parents' voices, partly because my thoughts were driving me crazy. For a while, I watched a talk show in which some tweedy men with beards and glasses were arguing about the Brady Bunch. They kept on using strange words like "seminal" and "inscribed." When they weren't speaking, they were scratching their beards or rubbing their glasses with dirty handkerchiefs. I turned the channel when they got up, formed a kick line, and started singing: "It's a story of a man named Brady…"

I found my grandfather on the next channel. He was advertising his company. I knew the ad by heart, but for some reason I couldn't bring myself to turn the channel. He was wearing a tacky white jacket that he couldn't button shut over his belly and gesturing and shouting like a ringmaster at the circus.

"Camman down to Cardboard Box Emporium!" he shouted. "We got cardboard boxes in all colors, shapes and sizes for all your cardboard needs. Take exit fourteen off the turnpike, Route two-ninety east three exits to College Square. You'll find us right across from the stadium. What are you waitin' for?"

CHAPTER ELEVEN

Most people can't stand my grandfather. They find him loud and obnoxious, bossy and cruel. But I've always liked him because he never pretends to be anyone other than himself. He swears and drinks and emits foul-smelling gasses even when guests or grandchildren are around.

When my father was growing up, Grandad was always broke. He had lots of crazy ideas about starting businesses, but none of them ever went anywhere. He tried importing canoes from Canada and shrimp from Bangladesh, growing Belgian endive, manufacturing costume jewelry, retooling tractor engines for use in windmills. One enterprise failed more miserably than the one before it, so the family had to live off my grandmother's earnings as a temporary legal secretary.

Grandad's big break came when he traveled to the Philippines for my parents' wedding. Most Filipinos don't use suitcases when they travel—instead, we use these giant cardboard boxes that can hold all the gifts you're expected to bring home when you travel.

Seeing all the boxes riding the conveyor belt at Manila International Airport was a revelation to Grandad. When he returned to Worcester, he mortgaged the house to launch his latest business. He started out with a trailer-load of cardboard and an ad on local TV. For some reason, maybe because of the recession, people in Worcester just went nuts about cardboard. They started using cardboard boxes for everything: laundry baskets, playpens, trashcans, toolkits, bookshelves, doll houses. Some people even lined them with plastic and used them for flower pots.

After a while, Grandad became this cult figure in town. He traded in his Ford Falcon for an only slightly newer purple Lincoln with suicide doors and drove around town honking and waving at people, handing out fliers for Cardboard Box Emporium. Once, he even ran for mayor and lost by a vote on the recount.

I was about to turn off the TV when Grandad stuck his hand out of the tube and grabbed me by the nose.

"I'd reco'nize that god-damned beak anywhere in the world," he growled. "What the hell you doin' just sittin' around like there's nothing to do?"

I didn't answer him. I knew he wanted me to go to work in his shop. He'd told me a hundred times that school was no place for a kid. The only place to learn anything worthwhile was on the job. He'd dropped out of junior high school, but now he was the president of his own company and a millionaire to boot.

I liked my grandfather, but I didn't like the idea of going to work for him. I squirmed and wriggled the way only a small, bony kid can, but it was no use. His head and upper body were hanging out of the screen now, and he twisted me into a half-nelson. I kicked at the TV, trying to knock it onto the floor. It fell, but it didn't come unplugged. I felt a sudden sharp pain behind my eyes as he pulled me through the screen; then everything went dark and the air was sucked out of my chest as I entered the vacuum.

When I woke up, I was lying on a sofa in Grandad's office, my head propped on a big red plastic ringbinder. Before I opened my eyes, I heard the sound of an old fan with a bent blade that clanked as it spun, keeping the beat to a song on a crackly radio: Frank Sinatra in love. Just as I sat up, the old man appeared with a Dixie cup full of water.

Dløn had rendered him perfectly, right down to the discolored left front tooth and his habit of rubbing his hands together like a greedy banker.

"You want a drink?" he said.

I didn't say anything, just held out my hand. The cup was cool, but the drink, of course was unsatisfying. I thought about the bottle under my chair in Manila, but that seemed hopeless. I had no idea how to use my real hands now.

"I got some work for you to do," Grandad said when I'd finished drinking. Then he led me out into the shop.

The air in the shop was hot and dense with swirling cardboard dust. Unmade boxes, folded flat, rose in blocks like skyscrapers in a new city, narrowing my view to a long dark passage. We walked up and down several of these alleys before we found the person that Grandad was looking for. There was a nervous rattling sound, like insect feet on linoleum. Then, suddenly, I saw a huge red-bearded man scampering down from the top of the five-meter pile of cardboard.

"This is Carl," my grandfather said, as if nothing had happened.

Carl was breathing heavily, and the veins in his neck were standing out like fat blue roots. His chest and arms were exceptionally hairy, almost furry, and he had glowing red eyes. When I offered him my hand to shake, he ignored it.

Grandad laughed. "From now on you work for Carl," he said. "You do whatever Carl tells you to do. Carl'll teach you how to work in the 'pigs.' That's something you'll never learn in school."

He mussed my hair before he left, and his hand was all warm like a piece of bologna left out in the tropical air. It was strangely comforting, the roll of his familiar palm on my brow.

Once Grandad had left us, Carl led me down a series of cardboard alleyways, walking with this fast, jerky gait that reminded me of a horse. I almost had to run to keep up with him. Finally, we arrived at the dock where four men in dirty t-shirts and jeans were unloading bundles of cardboard from the mouth of a giant trailer. Carl barely spoke, barely seemed capable of speech, yet somehow he made it clear that I was supposed to help these burly, dust-encrusted men, the smallest of whom must have weighed at least twice as much as I do.

For the first ten minutes in the pigs, I thought I was going to die. I couldn't breathe the air, and my hands were getting all scratched up from the sharp edges of the cardboard. The bundles were too heavy for me to lift, so I had to drag them along the floor of the trailer. For a while nobody said anything about this. In fact, nobody said anything to me at all. But I could tell from their breathing and the way they nudged me when we passed each other that they were starting to get impatient. When I complained, they laughed and called me a wimp.

Finally, Carl pulled me aside. "You're gettin' in the fuckin' way," he said, glaring at me with his evil red eyes. "I got a better job for you."

When I asked him what I was going to do, he took off down an alley, pausing momentarily to gesture with his head for me to follow. Galloping at his usual lunatic pace, without ever pausing to check if he was going the right way, he led me through a maze of intersections that all looked the same. I searched for markings on the boxes or the floor that might explain his ability to navigate so easily, but I couldn't find anything. Sometimes he turned so quickly that I was uncertain which way to go, but if I listened I could follow the strange rhythm of his footsteps. When we'd been walking for ten minutes without getting anywhere, I started to fear the worst. I'd heard enough of Lola's stories to know what kind of beast he was.

He stopped at last in a gloomy corner of the shop. "This is the break room," he said, opening the door to a narrow closet of a room, filled almost completely by a large couch and a couple of beat-up green metal filing cabinets. In the far corner of the room, there was an even smaller closet—a tiny cubby without a door on it. Carl had to turn sideways to squeeze by the sink and cock his head to one side under the eaves in order to take a piss. While he was emptying his bladder, he suddenly became talkative.

"It's lucky you showed up," he said. "This place ain't been cleaned in years."

Standing in the doorway of the break room, without even stepping over the threshold, I could smell the sickening ammonia stench of the bathroom. I pretended I hadn't heard.

When he was done with his business, Carl did not even bother to flush or wash his hands. He began rooting around the break room, looking under the couch, behind the filing cabinets, and in all of the drawers. Finally he produced a musty brown mop, a yellow plastic bucket, a couple of dry-warped sponges, a putty knife, and several bottles filled with liquids in different colors. He took the caps off each of the bottles and sniffed their contents before selecting one and dropping it into the bucket.

"After you get through cleaning," Carl said, pointing at the bathroom, "I'll see about getting some paints and stuff."

"What do you want me to clean?" I said, pretending that I didn't understand.

"The bathroom. Clean the fuckin' bathroom," Carl grunted, and the veins stood out in his neck and his eyes seemed as if they might pop from their sockets. Then he handed me my gear and shoved me in the direction of the little room.

Standing in the bathroom, looking at the black porcelain of the toilet, breathing in the stench of the place, I broke down. I turned around and threw the bucket at Carl.

"Grandad wanted me to work in the pigs," I said, trying not to sniffle.

Carl stood in the doorway, his arms folded over his chest. "You can't work in the pigs. You just get in the way," he said. "You're going to clean the fuckin' bathroom."

I was furious. I had never cleaned a bathroom in my life, and I had never heard anyone use that word, fuckin', so often. I wanted to say something that would put him in his place, something so he would know just how stupid he sounded. At Lola's house, we had a maid to clean the bathrooms. No sooner had I finished taking a shower than she'd be in there mopping the floor and changing the towel. If I was sitting on the throne and I needed toilet paper, all I had to do was call.

"I can't clean the bathroom," I said. "I don't know how."

"Well, you're going to fuckin' learn," Carl said. He didn't seem to notice that I was crying, or if he did, he didn't care. He righted the bucket that lay at his feet and poured in some of the liquid from the bottle. Next he placed the bucket in the sink and began to fill it with water. "When the bucket is full of water, dip the fuckin' mop in and use it to mop the floor. Once the floor is wet, you can start to fuckin' scrape it." Now he opened the top drawer of one of the filing cabinets and pulled out a black plastic bag. "Put the garbage in here." He shook the bag and dropped it on the couch. "I'll be back to check in a few minutes. If you're goofing off, I'll stick your fuckin' head in the toilet and make you lick it clean."

I thought about running away, but I didn't have any idea where to go. Outside the door of the break room, the cardboard alleyways spread like a rat's maze. I was sure if I tried to escape I would just get lost or worse, I'd run into Carl and he'd eat me. I even started wondering about whether or not there was any way to bail out of Dløn. Maybe I could get my fingers onto the keyboard and reset the system or give a command that would pop me out of the network. But doing that would have meant going against everything I believed about playing: once you locked in, you were committed. If you didn't stand by that, then you might as well stop playing. Anyway, who could say if I would ever get another crack at Dløn? And what if Bri really did need my help?

After a while, when I realized I didn't have any choice, I just gave into the work. First, I dumped the liquid from the bottles that Carl hadn't given me into the toilet to mask the stench. Then I started working on the floor, which was covered with a moldy green film. It was only as I started to pull up chunks of it that I realized it was newspaper. There were layers and layers of it. Under the corroded, fungus-infested top layers, it was hard and yellow, like *papier-mâché* varnished with mucus. To keep my mind off of what I was doing, I tried to read what was written on the newspapers. But none of the pages were clear enough to read: I couldn't even make out a single word or letter of the alphabet. It was as if it had all been printed with a hopelessly out-of-focus enlarger.

When I stared at the newspapers too long, strange things started to happen. A face would appear and then melt suddenly into another. It was like watching an ad for Benetton or a CNN news report. One moment, I was looking at Boris Yeltsin, then it was Mike Tyson, Yitzhak Rabin, King Hussein, Princess Di, Bill Clinton, Jesse Jackson, Fidel Ramos, Elizabeth Taylor, Nelson Mandela, Vladimir Zhirinovsky, Deng Xiaopeng, O.J. Simpson—as if all events in the outside world could be reduced to a kaleidoscope of smiling faces.

If I ignored the newspapers, I found that I could get into this rhythm where my body was doing the work while my mind was floating around somewhere else. As I scrubbed the toilet, using the mop handle and one of the sponges so I wouldn't have to put my hands in the filthy water, I pondered all kinds of strange notions. I wondered if Dløn had been invented just for me. Maybe someone was using Dløn to get revenge on me. Maybe it was Bri or the system manager of Apeiron. If not, I wondered why they'd bothered with my grandfather's shop. I wondered if everyone's experience of Dløn was just as personal. If so, did Dløn contain everything?

I wondered if Bri was really in another part of Dløn. Maybe he was talking to Marco now or visiting with the mermaids. Or, maybe Dløn was entirely different for him— maybe it was like one of those pick-your-own adventure books: only in this case, the choices were infinite. If adventures in Dløn were distinct for each player, it was hopeless to think that we would meet. Maybe it was stupid to imagine that Dløn was a place: Dløn was not a place but a time— right now. And maybe right now for me could never be right now for Bri.

In this way, letting my mind wander, I cleaned the floor, the toilet and the sink. I was just getting started on the walls when someone shouted, "Coffee! Coffee! Break time!"

Suddenly the floor was pounding with the sound of feet, and the guys who'd been working in the pigs came rushing into the break room, filling the air with their shouts and the sour stench of sweat. Two of the biggest, sweatiest guys stormed into the bathroom before I had a chance to get out of the way. One complained in a hoarse voice that the toilet was still dirty.

"I still can't see my fuckin' reflection," he said.

But he dropped his pants around his ankles anyway and sat down on the can. The other one ran the water in the sink, filled his hands and slid them over his face and hair, slicking black bristles behind his ears. When I tried to edge past him, he stuck his fat butt out till it touched the wall and trapped me. He didn't say anything, but I could see from the way he was squinting that he thought it was funny.

"Hey Leo, Leo the Lion," the man on the can grunted. "Where's the toilet paper?"

I looked at him: he was smiling stupidly. The toilet paper was on the hook, not two inches from his right hand.

"The same place it always is," I said.

"Give me some fuckin' toilet paper, Leo," he whined. "Come on Leo, little Leo."

"Get it yourself," I said.

"Leo, Lee-ee-ee-oh," he sang in a cheesy imitation of Harry Belafonte. "Give me some paper, so I can wipe me butt."

Fat Butt, still leaning over the sink, still running his hands over his face and through his hair, giggled, "That's a good one, Paul."

"Come on, Leo," Paul said.

I grabbed the roll and pulled off a few sheets.

"I need more, Leo," Paul said, whining and wheedling, like he was trying to seduce me. "Be a sweet child. Give me more."

The stench was unbearable. I felt tears starting to form in my eyes. More than anything I didn't want those assholes to get the satisfaction of seeing me cry. I was unwinding a big wad of paper, when Paul screamed and leaped off the can, bumping his head on the ceiling and starting a scuffle with Fat-Butt. In the confusion, I crawled into the space under the sink.

What happened next was simply beyond all reason. A rat the size of a tiger leaped out of the toilet bowl and chased Paul and Fat-Butt into the break room. I felt the slap of the rat's wet rope tail against my cheek as he rushed into the break room, but fortunately, he didn't notice me. From my hiding space, I watched him devour Paul, who had fallen on the floor with his pants around his ankles and blood dripping down the pasty white skin of his legs. The rat eviscerated the carcass with its sharp front teeth but ate only the stinking innards.

I was too frightened to move or make a sound. I had no sense that this was a virtual rat or that Paul was only a character. I was certain that if I did anything to attract the rat's attention, I would be the next to go. When the rat had finished mauling the carcass, he rose onto his hind legs and sniffed the air almost daintily. I felt a surge of adrenaline in my spine, and I had to clench my fists to keep from rushing him. Maybe he sensed something, because he cocked his head and looked in my direction for a terrifying moment. The face and gestures were familiar. His left front tooth was discolored, and he was wearing glasses. When he rubbed his hands together in a greedy way, I recognized him. It was Grandad. He seemed to smile at me before scuttling off into the shop.

I knew that it was bad idea to stay in the break room because once the rat was finished in the shop, he would no doubt come back this way. I stepped gingerly around the carcass, glancing at it only once, quickly. He looked like a jelly donut with the filling squished out.

In the cardboard labyrinth, it was easy to see which way the rat had gone. He left wet footprints and tailmarks on the cardboard, and every twenty meters or so I stumbled across a hard brown pellet the size of a baseball. My first thought was to follow his trail, because at least then he wouldn't sneak up behind me. I got the idea from a documentary on gazelles. Apparently, gazelles will follow a lion just so they know where she is. The announcer explained that a predator is only dangerous when you don't know its whereabouts.

Every now and then, I heard the sound of feet pounding in the distance followed by the rough scuttling and rush of the rat. Then someone would scream. Without seeing a thing, I could tell what was happening. The rat was chasing them around the maze like PacMan, systematically munching up the little goblins. I knew that rats had no aversion to eating their own young; if I did not come up with a new escape plan, it would only be a matter of time before he got hold of me.

Remembering that I had first seen Carl scampering down one of the piles of cardboard, I decided to try my luck at climbing. In class, Dr. Jack had once asked how many of us liked to climb trees, and no one had raised a hand. None of us had ever tried. It wasn't that I'd never had the chance. The idea had just never occurred to me. Why would you climb a tree? I had to hold my nose to keep from laughing aloud when Dr. Jack started telling stories about the trees he'd climbed. His voice cracked when he spoke of acacias with thick branches and broad crowns, whippy rubber trees, and the mangoes with tart green fruits you ate until you were about to burst. After he finished his story, he said that he felt sorry for us because we weren't really children.

As Fergus, I would have had no trouble getting to the top the pile. A leap and a scamper would have been enough. Now, I wished that I'd taken Dr. Jack's advice and learned to climb. I found that I could slide my fingers in between the sheets of cardboard, but getting a foothold was much harder. My feet skidded and slipped, and twice I fell from a height of nearly two meters. The second time, I bumped my elbow, and a pain zipped down to my finger tips. I was about to give up when I heard a scream a few meters away on the other side of the wall I'd been trying to climb. The rat was so close I could hear it chewing, sucking guts, and licking its hideous chops.

Now desperation was my teacher. I discovered that I could wedge my feet into the rough nylon strapping that kept the sheets of cardboard together. Although my right arm and hand were numb with pain, I managed to make my way to the top of the five-meter wall. After heaving myself onto the ledge, I made the mistake of looking down. The rat was there, sniffing the ground in the place where I'd fallen not two minutes before. I resisted the temptation to spit on him, and after a moment he scuttled off after some other prey.

CHAPTER TWELVE

When I stood up, I wasn't in the warehouse anymore. I was in the rainforest. I could hear birds chattering, water dripping, and insects scratching their wings: a bright keening sound, high-pitched like the isolated crackle of tinfoil against a microphone. The air was cool and damp and smelled like rain.

I was congratulating myself on having escaped the rat when I noticed Carl snuggled under a tree with a trunk three lanes wide and branches that disappeared in the mist of the canopy. His mouth was hanging open like an unzipped fly, showing off two rows of broad, flat horse teeth. And I had to admit what I'd been denying all along: Carl was a *tikbalang*.

I can't claim that I've been a good granddaughter to my lola in any way but one: I've always listened carefully to her stories. Even though I never thought that her advice would be useful, I took note of every detail. Now that I was face to face with the *tikbalang*, I knew exactly what to do. Of course, that didn't make it any easier.

The *tikbalang* sleeps very soundly. The only thing that will wake him is a sudden rustling or the scent of food. Even though Lola had told me that the *tikbalang* likes to eat little boys, I wasn't particularly interested in finding out whether or not a girl would do. I don't think I'd have dared to go near him if I hadn't felt confident that my scent was masked by the stench of the cleaners I'd been using.

I crept towards him, gingerly placing each foot so I wouldn't crush any leaves or trip on a vine. When at last I was standing next to him, I paused to work out my plan.

Even reclining with his back against the tree, the *tikbalang* was huge. His shoulders reached my chest, and his eyes were level with my own. I knew that if I made a mistake, I would end up stewing in his pot.

The trick, according to Lola, was to pluck three hairs from his back and then to jump onto his shoulders before he noticed. Two hairs wouldn't do it. Four meant disaster. My right hand was still tingling from the fall, so I had to rely on my left. Keyboarding is about the only thing I've ever done with my left hand. Now, it was shaking. I focused on three hairs that were sticking out from a bigger clump. They were bright red and thick as wire. I knew I'd have to pull hard.

On the first tug, the hairs didn't give at all. When the beast grunted and shuddered, I resigned myself to dying. Fortunately, I'd caught him by surprise, and I had just enough time to try again. This time the hairs came free with a jerk, and Carl, the *tikbalang*, was mine.

I don't know how I wound up on his back. But suddenly I was clinging to his shoulders and he was careening about, howling madly and bumping into trees, trying to knock me off. His shoulders were thickly muscled but his fur was mangy and bald in spots. He ran through the forest at an impossible speed. If I looked at the ground or the trees closest to me, I started feeling dizzy and nauseous. Closing my eyes only made it worse.

Otherwise, the ride wasn't what I'd expected. There was no grace or rhythm in his movements. He didn't feel like a real animal. He squeaked and lurched and jangled like one of those old mechanical horses you find at the mall, the kind where your mother puts in a quarter or a peso so she can fix her make-up while you get jerked around for a few minutes.

After a while, when we emerged from the forest onto a dusty highway, the ride became more exciting. The *tikbalang* dashed out among the jeepneys, pedicabs, motorized tricycles, giant rumbling buses and cars, as if he were just another form of provincial transportation. But unlike the occasional carts you saw being pulled by *carabao,* with long lines of traffic building up behind them, the *tikbalang* was the fastest thing on the road. When he reached a stalled bus, he jumped onto the roof, and continued at the same pace, leaving a trail of hoof-dents behind him.

Outside the forest, the landscape was rough and ruined: the fields were dry and dusty, baked yellow by the sun. The heat was like a dirty blanket that covered everything, making it difficult to breathe. We passed churches, chickens chained by the roadside, freshly harvested rice spread on the tarmac to dry, boys playing basketball at makeshift hoops, *carabao* sleeping in their wallows, sunk so deep in the muck that only their broad white horns were visible. Oddly enough, no one seemed to pay any attention to us. As we darted between the wheels of motorized tricycles in the towns, no one screamed or ran to the edge of the road to see us. Little children dancing the Macarena in front of their homes didn't miss a step. No men shouted. No dogs barked. No one threw anything at us. Maybe it was a commonplace occurrence: maybe people were always riding around on *tikbalangs* in this part of Dløn.

After a while it occurred to me that we were going so fast that they couldn't see us; indeed, things seemed to shrink and flatten as we passed them. In one town, I read the word *tubig* on a woman's lips and then a moment later, when we'd left her far behind, I heard her say the word in Spanish, *agua.* I wondered when we would reach the limits of Dløn, and I wondered why so much of Dløn looked like the Philippines.

Soon we turned off the provincial highway onto an unpaved road lined with rice and cane fields. The *tikbalang* slowed as he entered a shady grove where there was a collection of a dozen *nipa* huts built close together; maybe the heat was finally getting to him. Now he turned onto a narrow path, walking at a human pace. Beside a murky fish pond grew an old mango tree with a broad low crown, its branches sagging with the weight of hundreds of fat green mangoes. There, in the shade, the *tikbalang* kneeled like a well-trained horse and waited for me to dismount.

I don't know what came over me at that moment, but for some reason I couldn't resist the temptation to taunt the *tikbalang*. Standing three feet away from him, I licked the tips of the fingers on my right hand one by one, slowly, as if they were covered with durian juice. Fixing me with hungry red eyes, he began gnawing at his own shoulder and arm as if to make up for the fact that he could not eat me. Petrified, unable to pull myself away, I watched him suffer for several minutes until finally, overcome by exhaustion, he yawned, lay down at the foot of the tree, and went back to sleep as if nothing had happened.

I didn't have any idea of where I was or what I should do, but I knew that I had gotten everything I would from the *tikbalang*. I had overcome the monster, but who knows what tricks would happen next. The hollow beneath the mango was cozy and cool, but I didn't want to stay around.

Without giving the matter much thought, I decided I would continue along the path that had led us to the tree. Soon, I came out into an open space. There were fields stretching to the horizon in front of me. Freshly planted, stubby green stalks grew in neat rows in the fields. Off to the right stood a low ridge of mountains. Clouds were massed above it. Otherwise, the sky was clear.

The first hut I encountered was on the left side of the path. The walls and the roof were made of *nipa*—palm leaves woven together on a wood and bamboo frame. The hut was suspended on stilts just high enough for a fat black sow to squeeze under the floor when I entered the yard. The yard was neatly swept. Clothes were drying on a line hung between the house and a *rambutan* tree. The sight of the little red, prickly *rambutan* fruits made my mouth water. The scent of rice cakes hung in the air like a song.

I climbed up the stairs at the front of the hut and entered without knocking or pausing to call out. I'm not normally so rude, but I felt a strange sense of belonging, as if I had been doing it all of my life.

Even before my eyes adjusted to the darkness, I heard two women speaking in the corner of the room. My entrance didn't seem to bother them at all: they just kept on talking.

"The girl refuses to wear a dress."

"She runs around and fights like a boy."

"You can hardly call her a girl."

"Imagine wearing your hair that way."

They were speaking Waray, and I knew that they were talking about me. They were sitting on woven rattan chairs in the far corner of the room. On the table between them, there was a stack of sweet brown sticky rice cakes. I felt a deep hollow gnawing sensation in my stomach.

I walked over to the table and took one of the rice cakes. It felt sticky and gelatinous, and I knew how it would taste. Wondering how long it had been since I'd eaten, I sniffed the cake, but I did not taste it even though I'd begun to doubt Fra Umberto's advice about food in Dløn.

Meanwhile, the women continued talking as if I wasn't there.

"Anyway, her color's so strange that no boy will ever look at her."

"She goes around in the sun with her shoulders bare, and without a hat on."

"If only she were more like Bea."

I squeezed the rice cake so it oozed between my fingers. Even though I could not see their faces, I knew the women now. They were my mother's aunts, Lola Lunding and Lola Baby. Whenever they get together, they talk about what a disappointment I am. They do it in front of my mother, and they do it in front of me. They call me *"verde"*—the green one. They constantly compare me to my cousin Bea, my uncle's oldest daughter. She's sixteen and their model of Filipina girlhood. Her hair is perfect, straight, a shimmering cascade that always falls into place no matter how much she shakes her head. Her skin is Chinese porcelain. Her nose is tiny, a cute little hamster pug. To further the injustice, she has the one advantage I might have hoped to inherit from a European parent—she wears a size C cup while I dream of the day when I'll need an A.

Bea's in the choir at church. She spends her free time helping poor children. She designs her own dresses; her mother won't go out before consulting her about blush, eyeliner, or accessories. Bea's even a great student. According to her mother, she's never gotten below an A, even on a quiz. To make matters worse, she's modest and generous. She never brags about herself, and she always stands up for me. If I didn't hate her so much, I'm sure that I would love her.

After a while I sat down in a corner of the room, resting my back against the wall. If I didn't listen closely to what my aunts were saying, their voices merged with the chatter of the birds, the grunts of the sow, and the murmur of the river that ran behind the house.

I was beginning to get sleepy when the peace of the afternoon was interrupted by the sound of men singing. Startled, I ran to the door to see what was happening.

Soldiers were marching through the fields in formation. I could see them trampling over the young plants. They were big white men with moustaches. They wore cowboy hats and carried old-fashioned rifles on their shoulders. There were hundreds of them, and they destroyed the fields as they marched. One of them was carrying an American flag, waving it back and forth over his head, like a drunken fan at a football match. The scene was so frightening that I couldn't move from the door. Their song grew louder and louder, but it wasn't until they were about fifty meters away that I could make out the words:

Damn, damn, damn the insurrectos
Cross-eyed, khaki-assed ladrones
Underneath the starry flag
civilize them with a Krag
And return us to our own beloved homes.

While a person who doesn't know the classics is merely ignorant, one who doesn't know the history of her own country is a fool. That's what Dr. Jack said. I have two countries, and this was a moment in the history of both that I knew all too well. I felt as if I'd stepped into someone else's recurring nightmare. I knew precisely what was going to happen several minutes before it happened. To make matters worse, I also knew that this knowledge was useless.

I darted back into the room and tried to warn my aunts. But they just kept munching rice cakes and talking as if nothing in the world could be more important than their gossip. Several times I tried to interrupt them, but when I heard the soldiers' voices in the yard, I gave up and jumped out of the window at the back of the house. I thought about running out into the fields, but I would have been an easy target there. Instead, I held my breath and crawled under the house into the fat sow's lair.

The pig, who seemed just as frightened as I was, nuzzled up to me and began to snuffle miserably. I held it in my arms. It was the first animal warmth I knew in Dløn, and it was an odd sensation amid the sounds and stench. The pig's muzzle licked me, soft against my cheek, its fur not quite feral—almost downlike. The ground itself was wet and filthy, reeking of rotten garbage and shit. I could see the soldiers' disembodied legs darting about in the yard. It was like watching an old cartoon. They wore heavy leather boots that went all the way to the knee. They swore and shouted and shot off their guns.

After a while, I heard a strange rustling overhead and I thought I smelled smoke. I had the sense that something was burning. I heard my aunts scream, and then I saw their legs, sheathed in sayas, emerge amid the phalanx of the boots in the yard. My face stung with the heat. The pig squealed and ran outside. I looked up and saw a huge ball of flame. It was like being in the middle of a bonfire. At last, it got so hot I couldn't take it anymore. I scurried after the sow.

As soon as I emerged in the yard, a burly soldier grabbed me by the arm. "Look at the skinny little sow we got us here," said the soldier. "If you'd stayed in there any longer, we'd have been eating your tender ribs for supper." His accent was midwestern, slow and thick as barbecue sauce.

"If I'm a pig, you're a wart on my behind," I said.

The soldier laughed. "Where'd you learn to speak English?"

"Wherever it was, I learned a lot better than you," I said.

This seemed to be a sore point with the soldier. He jerked my arm behind my back, twisting and pulling so hard I thought he was going to break it. Holding me like this, he led me over to another yard where about two dozen women and children were sitting on the ground, guarded by five soldiers.

There, among the women, I noticed my lola. Unlike the others, she was sitting with her head held up, as if she had just finished ordering the maids to mop up a section of the floor one more time because she had noticed a speck of dust. My lola had always had the imperiousness of a provincial usurer, mistress of all she surveyed. She also looked suspiciously like the sow I had just run after, with scant porcine fur to prove it: her flesh kind of glowed among us.

She looked at all of us with contempt, mouthing something beneath her breath.

I noticed, without thinking it strange, that she was young. Lola looked to be about nineteen—a sweet *lechon de leche;* a milkfed girl. She was a plump, florid beauty: a Chinese damsel with proud cheekbones and droopy eyes. I used to try imagining her young but could never get the image. Beside her, we were all sallow, without distinction. I was made to sit down next to my aunts, who had finally run out of things to talk about. Lola, oblivious to us, seemed to be chewing or mumbling, a low breathing I had yet to locate fully.

We sat there for several minutes while groups of soldiers went from house to house, setting them on fire and waiting for the inhabitants to come out. The soldiers did this with the professional detachment of workers carrying out an essential service, as if they were plumbers or garbage men. The burning houses looked like props in a curious religious ceremony. The smoke burned my eyes and made my mouth feel dry.

My aunts were both fingering rosary beads and whispering prayers. At first I couldn't see exactly what Lola was doing, but as I sat there trying to get my bearings, figure out the outcome of these events, I realized I heard a song. It was an old one, lilting and convincing. My lola was singing.

My aunts wore the same spooky expression on their faces. I had seen it in the *Lives of the Saints:* the look of martyrs. On St. Sebastian, that pious pin cushion, it looked especially eerie. It made you wonder if those old ascetics knew what they were doing, or if they were just plain nuts.

Lola was now breathing close by my ear. It was a well-known intimacy, her stance when she told stories.

"Ibon mang may layang lumipad,
kulungin mo ay pumipiglas;
bayan pa kayang sakdal dilag
ang di magnasang makaalpas.
Pilipinas kong minumutya,
pugad ng luha ko't dalita,
aking adhika: Makita kang sakdal laya!"

She sang a song about longing and freedom and loyalty
and love. *Ibon mang may layang lumipad*....Bird of action,
bird of hope. Filipinos had sung this song in all the revolu-
tions—against the Spaniards, the Americans, and, only a few
years ago, amid yellow confetti in the Snap Revolt. The hymn
was now part of Filipinos like musculature, like bone. And it
was sung in the dry, hard tone of my grandmother's grand,
niggardly rasp, with the pinch of her waspish consonants
and her harsh, fallible grace. Hearing the voice of my grandmother, so true and right in Dløn, I wept for the first time,
as my country went up in flames.

There wasn't a single man among us. Most of the women
were old and feeble like my great-aunts. I was one of the
oldest children. But I knew that wouldn't keep them from
shooting us. Murdering children and old women had all been
part of President McKinley's approach to democratizing the
Philippines. He'd called it benevolent assimilation and
claimed that God had inspired him with the idea.

After Dr. Jack had told me about the Philippine-Ameri-
can War, I'd read everything I could get my hands on about it.
It made me feel sad about being a Filipina and ashamed of
being American. One American general, Jacob Smith, had given
the order that his troops were to fire on anyone over the age of
ten. "I want no prisoners," he'd said. "I wish you to kill and
burn. The more you kill and burn, the better you will please

me." But it was Lola who'd told me about the massacre on the bridge in her hometown. Her lola, who was thirteen when it happened, was the only one who had survived the shooting.

I found myself wishing that the soldiers had tusks or horns or some other deformity. I wanted them to be ogres so that I could hate them mindlessly and blame their actions on their inhumanity. I wished that they didn't speak my language or have beautiful teeth like the man who led us to the bridge and blindfolded us so we wouldn't look into the soldiers' eyes when they shot us.

It surprised me that none of the children were crying. Maybe they didn't know what was happening to them. I wished that I didn't know. I hated being reminded of the cruelty of history. And I hated the idea that all of these people were just props in an elaborate reenactment. I didn't care if they weren't really going to die. I knew that it had happened once, and that was enough. Even if it was just a game, it was still horrible.

Right before they put the blindfold on me, I looked at the sky. A hundred years of cloud formations passed overhead in three seconds. Crisp cirrus clouds were painted onto the stratosphere, great piles of stratocumuli gathered then dissolved instantly, churning cumulonimbi darkened the sky, and it began to rain.

When the guns went off, I remembered Lola's story. The shooting was supposed to provide an example to the rebels in surrounding towns. Lola's grandmother was only shot in the arm, but she fell off the bridge with the rest of them. She floated downriver and dragged herself ashore several kilometers away.

When the bullet grazed my right shoulder, I let myself fall.

CHAPTER THIRTEEN

The water in the river was strangely warm. I floated face down, fighting to hold my breath. My heart was pounding in my ears, and I thought I was going to drown when I finally raised my head and gasped for air. I thought I recognized Lola Lunding's *saya* snagged on an overhanging branch. But the current was so strong I didn't get a second chance to look. I hated my great-aunts, it's true—but I didn't want them to die.

Bouncing between rocks and the corpses of my ancestors, I thought about revenge. My first idea was to come back as Fergus and napalm the bastards. I pictured cowboy hats bursting into flame, Krag repeating rifles melting into puddles filled with singed moustache hair. But I knew that this would accomplish nothing.

If I were to go back, it would be as a guilty conscience. I would invade President McKinley's dreams with images of women and children being raped and chopped into little pieces. I would keep him awake all night, a howling wilderness in his head, until he realized that there's nothing benevolent about assimilating a people who had no wish to be assimilated.

The river turned a bend and broadened gradually. The current seemed to flow more slowly, as if the water had suddenly become viscous. I raised my head and floated with my feet in front of me, so I could bounce off of any obstacles I encountered. The water looked red, and it had a strange salty taste. When I realized that I was floating in blood, I panicked for a moment. I splashed and swallowed a whole mouthful. I tried to swim ashore, but the embankment was much too steep.

After a while, the river began to meander through a forest of low scrubby plants with no fruits or flowers, only paisley-patterned leaves in washed-out colors. The embankment was not as steep here, but the plants grew thick as mangroves right down to the water's edge. The heat of the river and the slow, throbbing current made me feel sleepy. I was desperate to get ashore.

Finally, I dragged myself up onto a little stretch of beach on the left bank where there was just enough room to stand beneath the thicket. When I first tried to get up, my knees buckled. My clothes were soaked through and heavy with clotted blood. My skin was itchy and shriveled. When I tore a leaf from one of the plants to clean myself I heard a scream.

"Why'd you do that?" someone said in a bubbling voice, as if she were speaking through a mouthful of water.

I looked around, but I didn't see anyone. "Who said that?" I said.

Drops of a black, gummy substance dripped onto the ground from the branch where I had torn off the leaf, and new plants sprang up immediately, their leaves unfolding in the same cheap upholstery pattern, repeating in miniature the form of the first plant.

I heard the voice again. "I know you don't recognize me," it said, hissing like a green log on a fire.

The voice sounded familiar. "Emily?" I said.

There was a silence. More liquid oozed from the plant. More plants sprouted on the beach.

"I wish you hadn't recognized me."

"Where are you?"

"The plant," she said.

I looked at the leaf I was holding. It was soft and pliable like skin, but it was covered with the same sticky resin that was dripping from the stem of the plant. It wouldn't do any good to wipe myself with it, so I dropped it.

"You're a plant," I said. I wasn't surprised. Nothing surprised me anymore. "I miss you."

"I miss you too."

Emily had been my friend in seventh grade. After I moved away, she killed herself. I don't think she did it because I moved away—she had lots of other friends—but I felt guilty for months after I heard about it. I'd promised to keep in touch, but I hadn't e-mailed her or anything.

"I'm sorry I didn't write you," I said.

"That's all right," the plant hissed.

It sounded like she was angry.

After I found out about her suicide, I kept thinking it could've been me. It should've been me. She was a much better person.

Everyone respected her. Even the teachers were afraid to argue with her. At the age of twelve, she'd thought everything through. She'd studied Gandhi and Simone Weil. She was a vegetarian, and she wove the cloth she used to make her dresses. When she got into trouble it was because of her principles.

"Why did you do it?" I asked, hoping, I suppose, to be let off the hook.

"I'd decided that if you're not part of the solution, you must be part of the problem," she sputtered, and more of the black stuff oozed from her stem. New plants sprang up, and soon I was up to my knees in enough leaves to make a bargain basement sofa.

After a moment, Emily continued: "I didn't see myself as part of the solution. Remember how we talked about how privileged we were?"

"Yeah, you told me to give all my t-shirts except one to the Salvation Army," I said. "You said all we needed was one shirt, and we argued whether it was more wasteful to use all that soap for washing that single shirt or buying a new t-shirt and washing less."

"You always argued too much," Emily said.

"Factless arguments," I reminded her. "That was our bond."

"I kept thinking about the waste," Emily went on. "Every day, my family consumed twenty-five thousand calories of food, mostly in the form of refined grain products, processed dairy goods, and animal fats and proteins. Two hundred and fifty cubic meters of water per month, thirty thousand kilowatt hours of electricity per year. And I knew that in parts of Africa, there were whole villages that consumed less than we did. I kept thinking about that. And I wasn't having any impact on my family or community, never mind the world. It was just too depressing."

"But you're the one who convinced the school to start a recycling project. You got them to use energy-saving lights. You even made the canteen serve vegetarian meals."

"I did," she said.

"Do you really believe that you were part of the problem?"

The branch made a horrible hissing sound. It obviously cost her a tremendous effort to speak. "My mother found me dangling in my closet," she hissed. "My eyes were bulging, and I'd shit my pants."

"God."

"It was a stupid thing to do."

"I just can't imagine you doing anything stupid," I said. "I mean, you always saw through everyone's bullshit. The teachers were terrified of you. I remember when you convinced Mr. Lucas that doing rough drafts was a waste of paper. He couldn't say anything because your drafts were always so perfect."

"Sometimes that's a dangerous thing, seeing through the bullshit. Now, I wish I could see my way back into it. You have to be there if you're going to make it better. I just got so discouraged. I kept thinking about the way the world's population was growing, you know—and it was just too overwhelming."

I felt terrible. Emily had done so much for other people, and then when she'd needed help, no one had been there for her.

"How did you wind up here?" I asked.

"I don't know, but I'd rather be anywhere else. Actually, I'd rather not be at all."

It seemed a terrible punishment. Throughout her life she had struggled to reduce herself, to consume less, to take up less space, to make less demands on the environment. Finally she'd tried to destroy herself, but now she'd wound up in this place where she just kept spreading, endlessly reproducing herself. It occurred to me that the designers of Dløn were not merely evil; they were vicious.

"Can I do anything for you?" I said.

"You can tell me what you're doing here."

"I'm looking for a boy."

"That's no way to solve your problems."

"He's a friend."

"Is he short, with blondish-brown hair and a mole on the left side of his nose?"

"Did you see him?"

"No," she said. "A priest asked about him—a fat priest with garlic breath."

"Fra Umberto," I said. "Where did he go?"

"If I were you," Emily said, "I wouldn't bother with either of them. I'd get out of this place and stay out."

I told her about the shooting on the bridge and all the other stuff that I had been through. "I'm not going to give up now," I said.

Emily rustled her leaves as if she were trying to point at something. "I can't say exactly where he went. Try climbing the embankment. From there you should be able to see a church spire. That's where the priest said he was going."

"Thanks, Emily," I said.

The plant hissed, and I saw that a new leaf was growing where I'd torn the first one off. I wanted to hug her, but I knew that it was pointless. I'd probably just break another one of her branches.

The new plants had grown so quickly that the little patch of beach was covered completely in foliage now. Scaling the embankment, I did my best to avoid stepping on plants, bending or snapping their branches. But the weird paisley foliage grew as thick as a blackberry bramble, and there were places where I had to shove branches aside just to keep moving forward. My progress was accompanied by moans and complaints. When the leaves brushed against my skin, it felt as if someone were trying to hold onto me. It occurred to me that if I stopped I might never again see Fra Umberto or Bri, I might never get out of the bramble.

CHAPTER FOURTEEN

In the middle of a shimmering orange desert under a sky of blueberry syrup, the church, with its stained glass and stone filigree, looked like an abandoned wedding cake. It had flying buttresses, gables, pointed arches, a circular oculus above the central portal shining like a stained-glass mandala, and live gargoyles dancing about on the roofs and gutters. As I approached the portal, the gargoyles crouched and leaned out over the eaves to hiss at me, frothing at the mouth like rabid squirrels preparing to pounce. When this did not scare me off, the fiends went ballistic, hopping up and down and wailing, waving their arms, rolling their eyes, and baring their pointy little teeth.

Maybe I should have ignored them and run right into the church, but for some reason, the gargoyles provoked me. I felt like I had taken too much shit in Dløn without giving any back. I knew they were just putting on a show. They were at least twenty meters up. There was no way they were going risk a leap from that height. What could they do to me?

"Ineffable lechers! Incontinent paramours!" I shouted, trying to remember choice vocabulary from Dr. Jack's class. "Dyslexic cabalists! Lubricious heresiarchs! Foul and pestilent congregations of vapor!" Even though I wasn't entirely certain of what I was saying, I felt great, better than I'd felt since I'd started my journey in Dløn.

The gargoyles, of course, did not see the humor in my insults. Soon, they began to bombard me with feces. At first I watched them in amazement. A gargoyle would crap into one hand then maneuver himself with the other until he was dangling monkey-style from a buttress or parapet. Finally, he would take aim and launch his bomb. The little fiends aimed well, hurling the shit so hard it made a sizzling sound as it flew. Twice I was hit on the shoulder, and I felt one turd whizz by the back of my head. The stench was foul and swampy, like vegetables that have been left too long in the crisper.

No matter how hard I pulled and yanked, the door wouldn't budge. It was five meters tall and two meters wide and made of oak or some other heavy hardwood; its intricate carving depicted scenes from the Old Testament. I recognized Noah's Ark, Moses receiving the Ten Commandments, Jacob wrestling the angel, and Abraham setting out to sacrifice Isaac. Although the scenes were unmistakable, the holy men had the faces of cartoon figures. Noah looked like Popeye. Jacob was Underdog. And Abraham and Isaac had the huge Japanese eyes of Racer X and Speed Racer. I was examining a section of the carving in the upper right hand corner, standing on tip-toe and leaning against the cool wood, studying the look on Lot's wife's face as she was turned into a pillar of salt—a strange mixture of curiosity, defiance, horror, and Wilma Flintstone idiocy—when suddenly a missile hit me square on the cheek. It was hard as a snowball, but it exploded on contact, splattering into my eyes, making them burn and sizzle like Polyphemus's retina on the end of Odysseus's spit. Blind, I staggered and fell against the door.

Oddly, it gave against my weight, and I fell heavily onto a cold floor. As I lay there, writhing and clutching my face, I heard the swish of a dress and the clatter of approaching footsteps. I was sure that I was going to die. But that thought did not disturb me as much as it should have. My eyes felt as if they had exploded. I welcomed death as an escape from the pain.

I felt a hand on my shoulder. Then someone spoke. "My child," he said softly. It was Fra Umberto.

He lifted me onto my feet. But when he tried to embrace me, I wriggled away. I wasn't in the mood for some cheap display of affection. I wanted to put out the fire in my skull.

"Where have you been?" he asked calmly, as if we had just gotten back together after a holiday.

"My eyes are on fire," I said. "I can't stand here and make small talk."

"We'll take care of that," he said, taking me by the arm and leading me away. I could tell by the way our footsteps echoed in the otherwise still space that the church was huge and empty. We walked for what seemed like hours, during which time I remember thinking that I would be forever blind. I tried not to panic, but I couldn't keep from crying.

Fra Umberto whispered in Italian to comfort me. I do not remember what he said, but it was all very sweet and gentle. At last, when I thought I couldn't go any further, he stopped.

"Are you ready?" he said.

"Please."

"Hold your breath but keep your eyes open," he whispered.

Suddenly my face hit water and my head went under, too. It was cool and sweet-tasting. Three times, he immersed me, and after the third time, my vision began to return. I saw as if through a pair of sunglasses, but I saw. The huge soaring arches that met in the shadows of the vaulting, the light falling through the stained glass of the clerestory had a soothing effect on me.

After wiping my face with the hem of his habit, Fra Umberto held my hands and examined me. "Can you see?"

I nodded.

"You look like you need a bath," he said after examining me.

"It wouldn't hurt."

He smiled, showing handsome, evenly spaced, white teeth. "I'm sorry I can't offer you a proper tub," he said, pointing at the big stone tank filled with murky water. It reminded me of the tanks you see at fish markets, only it was divided by four metal cylinders that rose in the middle.

"This is a baptismal font from the 1300s. In those days they only baptized on Holy Saturday and Pentecost, so the priests would baptize hundreds of people at a time. They would stand inside the cylinders to avoid getting soaked. It's Holy Saturday. Prime is just about to sound." Fra Umberto paused for a moment, and then he chuckled. "Would you like to be baptized?"

I put my hand in the water. The water was murky; I could barely see my fingertips. "I've already been baptized."

"You're a mess. You should take a bath." He scratched his head. "Besides, I was hoping to practice. I've never baptized anyone."

"I told you I've already been baptized."

"It wouldn't affect anything. After all, I'm not really a priest. I just thought it might be fun to try."

"If you're so anxious to practice, why don't you baptize a gargoyle instead?"

"Well then," Fra Umberto muttered, sounding somewhat hurt. "I'll let you get on with your bath." But he stood there as if he intended to watch.

"I don't have anything to change into," I said.

He nodded, seeming pleased that I'd given him something to do. "You wait here. I'll get something," he said, and then he shuffled off towards the choir.

I undressed quickly and scampered into the baptismal font, afraid that he might suddenly return. The water reached my shoulders. At first it was so cold that I couldn't stop shivering. But gradually, as I scrubbed the caked blood, grassy waste, and other spoils from my elbows and knees, I began to adjust. When I felt I was as clean as I was going to get without soap, I rested. Wedging my legs between two of the cylinders, I floated with my hair in the water and my eyes closed.

Gradually the water began to warm up, and I smelled, faintly at first, the delicious *kinoki*-wood fragrance of a Japanese *furo* bath. I did not know if the transformation had actually occurred, but as the water became warmer and the scent more distinct, I didn't dare open my eyes for fear of discovering that it was an illusion.

Even with my ears submerged, I could hear the bells ringing for Prime. As the bells tapered off, someone began to sing a song in Latin, a lovely tenor soaring to the vaulting:

Gaudeamus igitur juvenes dum sumus
Gaudeamus igitur juvenes dum sumus
Post iucundam juventutem
Post molestam senectutem
Nos habebit humus
Vivat semper juvenes!

The song was beautiful. It felt holy and profound, as ancient and indecipherable as the stained glass windows and the tracery of the cathedral.

Fra Umberto seemed transported by the song. He closed his eyes and rocked on his heels. The wrinkles under his eyes seemed to smooth: he looked younger. I noticed for the first time that hiding under all the facial hair was a pair of beautiful, full lips.

When he was finished, I asked, "What was that?"

"A Roman drinking song," he said.

"Why did you sing it?"

"I don't want to forget it."

"But why not some other song?"

"One of the monks at the abbey used to sing this song. He would sing in the evening when he came in from the fields. I always found it uplifting." Fra Umberto seemed to hesitate. "Did you enjoy it?"

"It was beautiful," I said. "But I still don't understand why the monk knew a drinking song or why you decided to sing it for me."

"Giving Fra Andrea that song was someone's idea of a joke, I suspect—one of the petty sins of the designers. It was the only song we had at the abbey that wasn't somehow connected with our offices. In a way that made it all the more precious."

Now the water was cold again, and I was beginning to shiver. But I did not want to get out with Fra Umberto standing there. What if he was just an old cyberbator, and this whole adventure was a scheme to get me to take my clothes off? That would explain the singing.

Finally, I splashed him. "How long are you going to stand there spying on me?" I shouted.

"Careful," he said. "You'll wet your clothes."

"I don't care."

He started to move towards me. I screamed.

"Don't come near me."

"I just wanted to give you your clothes."

"Leave them on the floor," I said, pointing at a spot between us. "Then go away until I'm dressed."

"You're awfully squeamish," he said. "I'm just an old priest."

"You just told me yourself that you're not really a priest," I said.

At this, he laughed and put down the bundle he was carrying. "I'm sorry," he said. "These were the only clothes I could find."

When I was sure he was gone, I leaped from the font. The air in the church was cold and damp, so I dressed in a hurry. Fra Umberto had brought me a habit much like his own—a sort of thick cloth dress made of this itchy brown material. It was the most uncomfortable thing I had ever worn in my life, but at least I was warm and dressed.

While Fra Umberto was gone I thought about the way he had tricked me into visiting Dløn and then abandoned me. By the time he returned, I was fuming. "Where have you been all this time? Have you heard anything about Bri?" I growled.

"Bri?" he said, staring at me as if I were raving.

"Bri, the whole reason we're in this stupid place."

He nodded. "Well, to answer your first question. I haven't been anywhere. I don't exist in space. I am information, code, signs and symbols."

"Fine. What have you been doing? Have you found out anything about Bri?"

"I have a confession to make."

"Isn't it supposed to work the other way around?"

"As you said yourself, I'm not a real priest. I haven't been ordained. I can perform the ceremonies associated with the sacraments. I know the rituals and the prayers, but there wouldn't be anything sacred in the performance. If you confessed to me, for example, I couldn't really offer absolution for your sins. God, as far as I know, is not online, and if he is I don't know his e-mail address."

"Is that your confession?"

"Only a small part of it." He took out his handkerchief and began to rub his glasses. "I've been using you."

"What do you mean?"

"I had to crack Dløn. You were my key. On my own, I couldn't get in. Following you, it was easy."

"I'm hurt," I said sarcastically, hand over my itchy heart. "I thought you followed me because you loved me."

"Leonora Caccianemica, one day you'll find that someone loves you, and it will make you weep. In the meantime, mind your manners and be serious! Why can't you ever be serious?"

The monk's voice echoed in the cathedral. His visage was stern, and he looked almost disappointed.

I was embarrassed and daunted, and I shifted on my feet, my face turned away from him, as if I were not bothered.

"Why did you want to get into Dløn?" I asked.

The monk looked at me squarely.

"You remember I told you about the books that were disappearing from the library in Apeiron. I am Apeiron's librarian, and in a way, I am also Apeiron's library."

"You are both code and custodian?" I asked.

"You might say that," he said impatiently. "As Dløn was stealing things from the library, they were stealing bits of me. If I'd waited any longer, the library would have become a useless collection of disconnected and fragmentary information. And I would have become worse than useless. I would have become misleading."

"So what have you been doing in Dløn?"

"I've been snooping, trying to figure out what Dløn is and how it works."

"And?"

"Dløn is a system evolving into meaninglessness. Dløn is the process of unreason."

I wasn't sure I understood what he was talking about. "What is that supposed to mean?"

Fra Umberto smiled. "Compare Dløn with Apeiron. In the simplest terms, Apeiron is a receptacle. It is a place to store information. People who wish to use that information may visit Apeiron as they please and use the information as they will. Dløn doesn't work that way. Access, use, meaning don't matter in Dløn. The only purpose of Dløn is Dløn."

"So who's behind it?" I said.

"No one is behind Dløn. It is its own purpose—a sort of metaphysical puzzle, if you will. Dløn is whatever Dløn can get away with."

I wasn't sure if I believed Fra Umberto's metaphysical explanation. If he'd deceived me once, who was to say that he wasn't doing it again?

"Maybe you are the one behind Dløn," I accused.

"I wish I were."

"Why should we go on then—how do we fight something that is not, the system that is no system?"

"If you pull out now, you will be sorry."

"I'll lose Bri?"

"Not just Bri. Who do you think you are now?"

"Leonora Caccianemica, known in Apeiron as Fergus, *verde* to my relatives, brat, Filipino-Italian-American—"

"You are nothing outside of Dløn: neither fantasy nor Filipino. Not American or mongoose, you are unnamed. You entered Dløn and lost yourself. Right now, you do not exist outside of Dløn."

"You wanna bet? I'll take my headgear off right now and zap you with a click."

"Do that at your peril. You have to move on to retrieve yourself, as in any good mystery."

"What if I don't?"

"I can't vouch for the consequences."

"Your story, as you tell it, must serve somebody's interests," I said.

Fra Umberto laughed so the soccer-ball belly shook underneath his habit in a most annoying way. "Of course it does. Dløn serves the purposes of anyone who will make it serve them. You don't need a conspiracy to explain that. Think about it." Fra Umberto pointed at a shiny spot on his forehead and squinted so his eyebrows formed a single ridge of fur above his glasses. "You enter Dløn, imagining yourself a player, and meanwhile, Dløn processes you as a set of signs and symbols, as information, or, if you want to be crude, as a chunk of meat. It separates you from yourself. It inserts you in a process that is not you. In the end, someone is bound to make a bundle selling you—the you that is no longer you—back to yourself."

My head hurt from the diatribe. I hardly knew what Fra Umberto was talking about. It seemed to me that he was just avoiding the question. "I'd like to know one thing: Is Bri in here or is he not? Is he being processed?"

"It would appear to be so, but it's difficult to tell. And if you give up now—how will you ever know?"

I hated him when he had all the dead-on answers. My eyes were no longer stinging, but now I had a headache. "So what are you going to do?"

"We must continue. We must find the words that are missing, gestures that have been lost, signs that have been warped and maimed. We must stop Dløn from encroaching on the rest of our memory, the universe as we love it."

I looked at him. He looked almost ridiculous. He was pulling at his baldnesss, tearing out his hair where he had no hair. I guess I was moved for a simple reason: because he was. Maybe passion is the weak spot of an ornery child.

"Where do we go from here then?" I finally said.

"Good girl," the monk said. "I knew you'd see it my way."

Did I have a choice, I thought. I did not want to test his argument. I thought of what I had seen, what I had found and overcome. The soldiers in the forest. The gargoyles in the church. I thought of the plant who had been my friend. The entire mutating and abominable world of Dløn: it scared me to think I might stay here forever.

The monk continued: "Dløn is not an environment like Apeiron where you have any power over what's going to happen. There's only one way to go. You follow the process. Think of it as a waterslide. We must surrender ourselves to gravity. And who knows—maybe we will find your friend."

A thought occurred to me. "Why don't you just destroy Dløn?""

"Two reasons," Fra Umberto grinned. "First of all, if we destroyed it we would lose everything that has been stolen from Apeiron. Secondly, we would never solve the puzzle."

"I thought you said it was meaningless."

"What a lovely mind!" Fra Umberto patted me on the cheek fondly. "I said it was unreasonable and meaningless, but I didn't say there wasn't a solution."

"But now that you're in, what do you need me for?"

"Without you, I'd be detected in a moment," Fra Umberto's eyebrows twitched, the caterpillars dancing. "And you still want to rescue your friend, don't you?"

Fra Umberto's smugness annoyed me. Priests weren't supposed to be smug. "So, you're my guide, but I'm your shield?"

Fra Umberto smiled, showing all of those white teeth.

"Where to, Guide?" I muttered.

"It doesn't matter, really, not in Dløn. We just move."

"Wait a minute. Is that why you just stood there outside my window in Worcester?"

"What?"

"I tried to move towards you, but it was like I was stuck in one of Zeno's paradoxes. I couldn't get closer. And you just kept walking back and forth as if you hadn't noticed."

"It wasn't me."

"Are you you?"

Fra Umberto's eyebrows twitched like hideous insects. "We shouldn't linger," he said. "I thought I had avoided detection."

"As soon as you get what you need, you're going to crash Dløn," I whispered. "Aren't you?"

"If I have to."

"And if you're not crashed first?"

Fra Umberto did not answer my question, but the look on his face was answer enough. He took me by the arm and guided me through an arched passageway towards a vast open space where the light was much brighter. By now, my sight had almost returned to normal, but maybe things would have been better if I had remained blind.

CHAPTER FIFTEEN

The nave of the cathedral was as big as an indoor arena but more austere, with great stone arches disappearing into the smoky green light of the vaulting. I thought I smelled incense. The dense greasy scent made me feel dizzy. If Fra Umberto had not been holding me, I would have collapsed on the floor, but he was able to maneuver me deftly into one of the pews.

I must have blacked out for a moment, because when I sat up again, everything had changed. Where before the nave had been filled with the spooky, breathless silence of an abandoned place, it was now thick with homey noises. I heard gurgles and snorts, coughs, sneezes, oozing burps, farts, whispers and giggles, rustling dresses, tapping feet, squeaks, thumps, mumbles, moans, laughs, cries, gasps. And I saw that there were children everywhere. Infants were crawling on the floor and sleeping on the benches. Toddlers were playing with the hat clips, making them slap against the backs of the benches, or rocking on the kneelers. There were children of every age, ranging from infants so small you'd be afraid to hold them to kids about my age.

I don't really like little children. I never know what to do around them. I think they can sense it, so usually they leave me alone. But now, one girl about four or five years old, with messy brown curls, cute except for a hideous Pinocchio nose, padded up to me and tugged at my robe.

"I can tumble," she said. "Do you want to see me tumble?"

115

I looked at her without speaking. She was dressed in a jumper and sneakers. Her eyes were intense and bright. She radiated confidence and curiosity.

"I can dance too. I can dance the big gorilla or the ptero-dactyl." She extended her arms and began to hop from foot to foot.

I recognized her now. It was a dance that my babysitter had taught me when I was four. "Who taught you that?" I said.

"Silly goose," she said, placing her hands on her hips. "You know who."

"What's her name?"

"Do you want to play a game?" she said.

I did not want to play a game. I wanted to lie down and sleep. I wanted something to drink. I wanted to get out of Dløn. I wanted her to answer my question. "Don't you re-member her name?"

"Remember," she giggled. "Don't you want to play a game?"

I shook my head. The girl, seemingly frightened by my tone of voice, wandered off into the crowd.

I studied the children. All of them looked the same. They had curly hair, brown eyes, and long noses without bridges. Their torsos were long and thin, their legs somewhat stubby. Their skin had a weird greenish tint that I attributed to the incense. They were all short. Although many of them seemed to be about my age, none of them were taller than I. It was a parade of embarrassments. I was four in braids and batik dresses; I was six in overalls and a ponytail; I was eight in leotards; I was ten, unkempt in a grungy tie-dyed t-shirt; I was thirteen with a brand-new fade, jeans, and hiking boots. There were so many of me I couldn't even count them.

I was jolted when suddenly Fra Umberto spoke to me. "Do you recognize them?"

I did not want to talk to him. I no longer trusted him. He had told me before that Dløn was an effect of Apeiron. Maybe this was just another one of his games or tests. Maybe he was experimenting with children to see what it took to make them crazy.

"Do you want to talk with any of them?" he said.

I didn't answer. I watched as one little girl, a six- or seven-year-old, climbed up onto the back of a bench and began to walk, holding her arms out for balance. Another girl followed, and another. Soon there were dozens of girls performing on the benches. They did cartwheels, flips, and handstands.

Fra Umberto seemed enthralled by the performance, but I couldn't stand to watch. I noticed that none of the older girls were performing. If they watched, they made no effort to conceal their disgust. I'd quit gymnastics after second grade. My father had always been my biggest fan. I think he enjoyed my performances more than I did. I was in second grade when the divorce was finalized. I think he really just wanted to get rid of me. We were living in Lima then. Anyway, gymnastics was becoming a job instead of a game. I was practicing so much I hardly had time for anything else. If I stayed up after supper messing around in virtual reality, I wound up falling asleep in class the next day. Halfway into the season, I just quit. The coach kept trying to guilt-trip me into coming back. Finally, I sent his e-mail address to a kiddie porn bulletin board just to get him off my back. When I think about it now, I know that it wasn't fair. My coach wasn't a bad guy; it was my father that I hated.

Fra Umberto nudged me. "Don't you want to talk to some of them? It might be interesting."

I didn't say anything, but I didn't interfere when he tapped on the shoulder of a girl sitting in the pew in front of us. "What are you doing?" he said.

"I'm thinking."

"What are you thinking about?"

"I'm thinking about why we have to die."

I didn't want to listen to her anymore. When I was eleven, I was morbid. I thought about death all the time. I wasn't suicidal. I was terrified by the idea that I might die before I figured out why I was alive. I had been reading a lot of poetry: Sylvia Plath, Ann Sexton, Robert Frost, Emily Dickinson, and Edgar Allan Poe. It was Edgar Alan Poe who saved me from going crazy. I would sit in my room and read his poems aloud for hours. After discovering the poem "Leonora" and spending a week memorizing it, I changed my name to Leo. I decided that the name Leonora was a curse, a name for an old aunt or a dead person. Leo, on the other hand, was dangerous and confusing. I started wearing my hair short. I refused to wear dresses. I became Leo.

I felt sorry for this person in the baby-girl dress and loafers. I wanted to tell her that things were going to get better. But then it occurred to me that maybe she would be eleven forever. Maybe each of the little Leonoras was stuck where she was. This thought made me feel awful. Being eleven forever would be worse than death.

After the eleven-year-old Leonora turned her back on us, Fra Umberto became antsy. "Let's get going," he said, standing up suddenly.

"Where?" I said.

"Onwards."

"Before we go any farther, I want you to explain this," I said. "You're supposed to be my guide."

Fra Umberto scratched his nose and looked at the ceiling. I knew he didn't want to talk. "What would you like me to explain?"

"What are they doing here?" I said, waving my arm so he could see that I meant all of the children.

"Technically, they aren't here."

"I knew you were going to say something like that."

"I don't understand it entirely myself. Why don't you ask one of them?"

"Which one would you suggest?"

"Ask one of the older ones."

I looked around. I saw a girl with a ring in her right lower lip. The lip looked red and tender. She was thirteen. I had taken the ring out before moving to the Philippines because I kept getting infections. Sometimes, it hurt so much I couldn't eat or drink anything but rice and water. There was no point in talking to her. I didn't trust her judgment.

Following Fra Umberto, I began to walk up the aisle towards the apse of the cathedral, all the while searching for a fourteen-year-old incarnation of me. We'd gone about twenty meters, stepping over children who were playing or sleeping on the floor, when one little brat grabbed hold of the hem of my habit. I tried to shake free of her, but she was stubborn and strong. Using my pocket as a handhold, she attached herself to my leg like a cast. The more I shook her, the more tightly she gripped me and the louder she giggled. I didn't want to hurt her, but I did not know how else to get rid of her.

"Try tickling her," someone said.

I looked in the direction of the voice, and it was like looking into a mirror. She was even wearing the habit.

"Who are you?" I said.

"I'm you two minutes ago."

"And the others," I asked, gesturing at the crowd.

"Ten minutes ago, half an hour, last year, the year before—you at every moment."

"What are you doing here?"

"I could ask you the same question."

"And I wouldn't be able to answer?"

She nodded.

"You're not much help," I said.

"Nor are you."

Her smugness irked me. "Do you always wear that ridiculous outfit?" I said.

She laughed. It was my most embarrassing laugh, a snort really. I suppress it in public. I take huge precautions not to get caught out by an unexpected joke. When there's no escape, I cough to hide it. "I hate your laugh," I said.

"I know you do."

"Do me a favor," I said. "Bug off. Disappear. You're bothering me."

She laughed again. Now the child was trying to climb up onto my back, using the chord around my waist as a foothold.

"Give me a piggy-back," she shouted in my ear.

I placed the palm of my hand firmly on her face, spreading my fingers as if to grasp a volleyball, and gave her a shove. She slipped and fell awkwardly on the stone floor. For a moment, she just looked at me, staring with big surprised eyes. Then she began to cry. It started as a grumbling in the belly but quickly blossomed into a full-blown, throaty howl.

Some of the girls in the pews muttered and sneered at me. One of them, an eight- or nine-year-old, took the baby in her arms and began to coo at her. Soon, the baby stopped crying.

"You could have tickled her," said my reflection.

Her advice didn't interest me. "You still haven't answered my question," I said.

"I don't know how to answer your question."

"Who takes care of you? Who feeds you?"

"You should ask someone younger. I've only been here a few minutes."

"Where were you before?"

"The same place you were."

I felt like smacking her, but I knew that a fight would be a no-win situation. I hadn't gotten any stronger in the last few minutes. "How can you be such a pain in the ass?" I said. That was the question my stepfather used to ask me when I got on his nerves.

The girl crossed her arms and stuck out her jaw the way I do when I'm angry. I knew there was no point in talking to her now. She would keep quiet just to spite me. No doubt she was thinking about some way to get revenge. That's how my mind works.

"You have a ridiculous nose," I said. "You look like Pinnochio, only he at least had a bridge to support the woodwork. You'll never have a boyfriend, because no one will ever be able to reach your lips to kiss you. Anyway, you have a boy's body and skin the color of moss. You're too short, and your legs are stubby. You have no sense of style. Your eyes are squinty. You're a nerd, a snob, and you laugh like a donkey. You're mean and vindictive. You ruin everything you touch. Your parents don't even want you."

I was looking at my reflection, but I could see out of the corner of my eye that other girls were pouring into the aisle from the pews, like hockey players taking the ice for a fight. Soon, there were hundreds of them in a tight ring around us, murmuring in angry undertones, staring me down, sneering, sticking out their sharp little jaws.

I am sure that they were just about to pounce and tear me apart when Fra Umberto grabbed me by the hand and dragged me away through the crowd. With his free hand, he pushed the girls out of the way and cleared a path all the way to the apse. They clawed at me and ripped my habit, but we moved too quickly for them to stop us.

There was an opening like a manhole in the center of the floor in the apse; without warning, Fra Umberto jumped into it, and I came tumbling after. Looking back up past the gaping faces of our pursuers, I saw that we were in the great open space at the center of the atrium, floating in the alphabet soup, and that what I had originally taken to be the ceiling of the atrium was actually the dome of the cathedral.

CHAPTER SIXTEEN

We fell as if through molasses. If we had passed a shelf with a jar of peanut butter and a loaf of bread on it, I would have had time to make myself a sandwich and return the jar to the shelf before continuing my fall. Fra Umberto—supine, hands joined behind his head, elbows extended—looked as if he were lazing on a hammock. All he needed was a glass of lemonade and a good book.

At first I was nervous about the symbols that were floating around us. It seemed that if you bumped into one, the consequences could be serious. But the fact is that they were about as substantial as clouds. You passed through them or they passed through you. It was impossible to tell how it worked. Once I watched something vaguely resembling a Hebrew gimel enter Fra Umberto's belly only to emerge moments later from his backside, without any noticeable damage to the priest or the sign.

Of course, it may have been his collision with the symbol that roused Fra Umberto from his reverie and inspired him to talk. At any rate, once engimeled, the old priest began to sermonize.

"You really shouldn't say those awful things about yourself," he said.

"They're true," I grunted.

"Not at all. You're a very pretty girl."

"There," I hissed. "I knew you were spying on me when I took my bath."

Blushing up into his bald spot, Fra Umberto looked almost boyish. "I wasn't spying on you. What makes you say that?"

"How do you know that I'm a girl?"

Fra Umberto laughed so hard he began to choke and had to sit up. "How do I know you're a girl?"

"Yes," I growled, unable to see any humor in the situation.

"We were recently introduced to your various incarnations from birth to the present. Now, assuming for a moment that your parents had the open-mindedness to allow a little boy to wear such an array of dresses, skirts, and Danskin tights, there remains the fact that you were born without any clothes at all."

"So you were spying on my childhood?"

"If one can spy involuntarily, then I was indeed spying. And I apologize with all my heart."

He seemed sincere, but I wasn't going to let him off the hook so easily. "What did you think before?"

"Frankly, I hadn't given the matter much thought."

"If you hadn't given it much thought, what is it that suddenly qualifies you to make an assessment of my appearance?"

Fra Umberto took off his glasses and began to rub them nervously. I wondered why his designer had given him this tic; it was not reassuring. "I judge your appearance in terms of classical principles. There is a grace and symmetry to your limbs and features. In your movements, I detect a harmony of the parts. All else is merely the fashion of the moment."

I hate it when adults tell me that I'm beautiful. If I am such a prize, why doesn't my telephone ring off the hook? Why don't I ever get asked to go to a dance or a party? Why don't I get flowers on Valentine's Day? It's not that I feel cheated; I just hate the hypocrisy. "Bullshit!" I said. "I have a ridiculous Italian nose in the middle of a flat Malay face. I have stubby legs. My ears are too small."

"I can only tell you my opinion."

"Great," I muttered. "So now I have a lovesick priest on my hands."

Now Fra Umberto seemed to become truly agitated. He slid the spectacles back onto his nose and seized my hand. "Although I am cursed with many appetites, the sexual one is, thank God or whoever created me, not among them. My affection is purely platonic."

"If that means you're going to sacrifice an animal to me, no thank you."

Fra Umberto blushed again. "The term *platonic* is generally used to signify pure intentions. My admiration of you stems more from your character traits than from your appearance. I admire the nimbleness of your mind, your critical bent, and your curiosity. I am impressed with your persistence. Most young people would have given up by now. You must care a great deal about this Bri."

"He's nice," I said.

Fra Umberto chuckled. "I should hope so. For the sake of this fellow, you've battled a giant rat, soldiers, and legendary creatures, swum through rivers of blood and feces, not to mention putting up with my divagations. I should hope so indeed." Fra Umberto smiled and lay back again on his imaginary hammock.

"Do you think we'll find him soon?" I asked.

"I haven't the faintest idea."

CHAPTER SEVENTEEN

I don't remember hitting the ground, and I do not know how I lost Fra Umberto. Sometimes being in Dløn made me feel like I was inside of an ADD kid's mind: a neuron fired, and suddenly I was off on another tangent. Still, I wasn't all that surprised to find myself sitting in a fold-out chair in a stuffy, low-ceilinged theater facing a stage where a man in a suit with a bushy green polyester wig, grease paint, and a big red grin painted on his face was prancing back and forth, singing an incredibly silly song. His gestures were all exaggerated, and his voice had an almost delirious lilt to it, which gave me the sense that he might lose control and burst into laughter at any moment. At first it seemed that he was just putting on a show, but as I watched and listened to the words, I got the idea that he was trying to sell something. He sang:

Oh happy happy happy happy
  Happy happy—Ho!
Oh happy happy happy happy
  Happy happy—Ho!

We're so happy when we're happy
And we're happy, yes we are!
We're so happy when we're happy
And we're happy, yes we are!

Oh happy happy happy happy
  Happy happy—Ho!

Oh happy happy happy happy
Happy happy—Ho!

With the melody still pouring from the overhead speakers, the big grin pranced to the center of the stage, bobbing his head from side to side and signaling for the audience to join him. "Come on, kids!" he said in his delirious voice. "I want you all to join in. It doesn't matter if you don't know the words. You can clap to the rhythm."

The audience needed no more prodding. They sang in loud, giddy voices. Looking around, I noticed that the seats and aisles were packed with kids, all of them wearing wigs and grease paint like the big grin. I decided they had to be characters. They seemed too stupid to be players.

The grin led them through two more rounds of the chorus; then, when they began applauding, he bowed melodramatically to the right, to the left, and finally, to the center. After the last bow, he remained frozen with his head down. He stayed that way for so long that I thought he'd gotten a cramp and couldn't stand up anymore. But when the applause finally fizzled out, he rose and waved to us.

"Thank you," he said, hyperventilating and panting with excitement. "Thank you. I know you're all very special people, and we're so happy to welcome you to the Community of Hronir. Before I tell you anything more about the community, I want you to take a look at the people sitting next to you. These are your new friends, your new family—the Hronir. Examine their uniforms."

I looked more closely than I had the first time. Everyone was wearing greasepaint: they had huge stupid smiles painted around their mouths and blue stars or red diamonds drawn on their cheeks. Their uniforms were baggy and bright, decorated with sparkles and giant polka dots. My pants were a shimmering violet, and my shirt an alarming shade of canary. My face felt stiff and greasy. With a growing sense of horror, I realized that they'd turned me into a clown.

"These uniforms give us our identity. They symbolize your commitment to the values of Hron," the big clown continued. "The Community of Hronir is based on four tenets, and I am confident that you will soon know them better than I do myself. These are the assumptions that all of us must share if we are to function as a community. First and foremost, we acknowledge that everything learned outside is false, destructive, and evil." Looking cruel in spite of the grin, he slammed his right fist against his open left hand as he said the words "false," "destructive," and "evil."

"Secondly, and this is my favorite," he proclaimed, rolling his shoulders as if his sportscoat didn't quite fit or as if he were getting ready to slug someone. "Every Hron always has fun. If it's not fun, we don't do it in Dløn."

Having reached one corner of the stage, he twirled theatrically and leaned forward to face the audience, his eerie red grin seeming to grow wider and wider. "The tenets of the Community of Hronir come from the heart. I know these tenets are true because I feel them in my heart." He thumped his chest. "They tell me to follow my heart, and my heart tells me that they are true."

Suddenly it occurred to me that I was back in school: the big grin was our principal, and the other clowns were my classmates. I've attended dozens of schools and virtual schools, all designed to shape you into the perfect citizen. Each of them was based on the idea that the child is a hunk of clay just waiting to be molded by some grand educational thinker. Above all things, these thinkers love lists. They brandish them with the mystical devotion of ancient wizards casting spells. If it isn't the four tenets, it's the five objectives, the seven themes, the twelve steps, the nine principles. Apparently, if you follow the steps or stick to the tenets, you're bound to attain a state just short of nirvana. I don't know: I always screw up somewhere in the process.

"The third tenet may be the most important tenet of all," the grin continued. "It is a tenet that speaks to every one of us. Remember that you must assume that all students, teachers, and administrators of the community, Hronir like yourself, always do the best they can." He sighed. "This is a truth I know you will cherish in your hearts."

"Finally," he said, holding his arms aloft, as if he were Moses receiving the final tenet from an angel hovering above him in heaven, "a Hron is free to question anything that has been learned on the outside. A Hron is free to speak out about mistakes, personal failings, problems, and shortcomings. The Hronir must not, however, question any of these precious tenets, for they are the foundation of our community. Without them, our community, our family will not function."

If my travels in Dløn should have taught me anything, it was when to keep my mouth shut. But I suppose that no matter where I go and how much I learn, I'll always be myself. When the big grin was finished with his speech, my hand shot up into the air as if it was spring-loaded. I guess he wasn't expecting any questions, because he took a long time about calling on me.

Though my heart was pounding in my mouth, I stood up so that every Hron would be sure to hear and see me.

"How do you spell Hron?" I asked, speaking as loudly and clearly as I could without shouting. "Is Hronir the plural form? And if it is, could you also please spell Hronir?"

I thought I heard a guffaw from someone behind me, but I didn't turn around, because I wanted the big grin to know that I was serious. Although it seemed a relatively simple question, he did not answer me immediately. He reached up to his tie and began adjusting it, as if he were having trouble breathing. Under the big red smile, I could see his real lips puckering, hard lines running from the corners of his mouth into the loose flesh of his jowls.

When he spoke at last, his voice had lost all of its bounce. It was like I had peed on his parade. "This is not the time for frivolous questions," he said. "No one wants to talk about nasty things like spelling, do they?" He put his hands on his hips, looked at the ceiling, and tapped his foot, as if he were waiting for an answer from an unbearably slow child. There was a vague murmur from the audience, and the grin returned. "Of course we don't. We're talking about the heart here. And spelling is so boring. Remember, if it's not fun, we don't do it in Dløn." He yawned. "I will forgive you because you have just come from the outside. I know you don't mean any harm."

I knew that I'd busted him. He was just as insecure and petty as the other happy, smiley thinkers I've met. It occurred to me that maybe the big grin really didn't know how to spell. He didn't seem to understand that I'd made a fool of him. After a moment, he did a little dance step, threw up his arms, and shouted in a frantic voice: "Come along, let's sing again."

And they did.

CHAPTER EIGHTEEN

Our schedules were color-coded. A blue dot meant a blue door. There were no clocks, but there were bells. When the bell rang, you found the next color on your schedule and looked for a matching door. My first class was behind a red door at the end of a long corridor that might have been in any school anywhere in the world. The walls and floors were green and lighted by flickering neon.

The classroom, on the other hand, was like none I'd ever seen before. It was laid out like a giant bed, with the floors and walls upholstered and cushions everywhere. There were neither books nor blackboards, no computers, rulers, pencils, maps, charts, pens, desks. Our teacher, Ms. Plammer, was as beautiful as a model or a character in a romance novel. She really had flaxen hair, a heart-shaped face, mysterious green eyes, and the delicate nose of a rabbit. She sat in the middle of the room, lotus-style, and smilingly introduced herself as we entered.

At first I studied each clown that entered the room. I was trying to figure out a way to tell if they were players or just characters devised by the author of my Dlønic nightmare. I thought that if I watched closely enough they might do something revealing. I had no idea what to look for, but I knew that I would miss the sign if I didn't pay attention.

Although I wouldn't have admitted it to myself at the time, I was also hoping that Bri would walk into the room. I was afraid that I might not recognize him under all the grease-paint if I didn't concentrate. I tried to study the faces beneath the make-up in a systematic way. I looked for details that couldn't possibly be concealed. I thought in terms of geometry. No amount of make-up can round the almond shape of an eye like Bri's. Some noses are triangles in profile and rectangles straight on. Others are pyramids or triangular prisms with globes perched on their tips. Faces can be oval, circular, ellipsoid, polygonal, even square sometimes.

I spotted many faces that were familiar, at least in terms of design. They were the faces of kids I'd been to school with in Beijing, Lima, Dar Es Salaam, Baltimore, Trieste, Worcester, Copenhagen, Ouagadougou, Marseille, and Brisbane. They were all kids I had known well enough to recognize, but whose names I couldn't possibly remember. Bri, of course, was not among them.

When I tired of studying faces, I watched for behaviors that might reveal something about the other clowns. I especially wanted to see if they tried to communicate with each other. Even the briefest smile might have meant something. It occurred to me that while the majority of the clowns were no doubt characters, there might have been a few other players in the room.

I was watching one clown, thinking that there was something distinct about his movements, a jerkiness, an unpredictability to his gestures that reminded me of someone in particular, when suddenly he shoved a finger the size of a swollen pickle into one of his nostrils and began excavating. When he noticed that I was watching, he smiled without interrupting his work, and his name flashed into my mind. It was Petey Cutting, terror of grade four and one of the most disgusting people I'd ever met in my life. It occurred to me that it didn't matter if he was a character or a player; either way, I wanted nothing to do with him.

When the room was full of clowns, Plammer finally addressed us. Smiling, making eye contact with each of us in turn, she explained that we were going to participate in a series of rituals that would help to initiate us into the Community of Hronir.

The first was a ritual renaming.

"We don't want anyone in the community to feel that they are less important than the others. Some of us come from the outside with some very strange names. Others come with names that are hard to pronounce. Some of us are attached to our names. Some of us hate our names. As a symbol of your initiation into the Community of Hronir, you will each be given a new name."

To begin the ritual she made us sit in a circle and hold hands. Walking around the circle, as if playing duck-duck-goose, Plammer promised to retrieve our names from the great sea of Dløn, which lay in the sacred region below the Community of Hronir. She had a brittle voice in the register of an oboe. Sometimes she squeaked, as if she'd cracked her reed. I kept looking around to see if anyone else was going to laugh. But, with the exception of Petey who kept smiling at me like an idiot, all of the clowns had their eyes closed.

It occurred to me that it must have been Plammer's voice that had kept her from becoming a spokesperson for fruit juice or getting a part on Baywatch. Of course, Plammer was not a real person, so the thought was ridiculous. I wondered why the inventors of Dløn would create someone like her. What did it mean when you had a character who looked great but squeaked like a broken oboe? Were you supposed to feel sorry for her?

When a name came to her from the great sea, Plammer would place her hands on a clown's head and intone, "Your Dlønic name emerges from the great sea. Rise to accept it, Ed."

As Ed stood up, the rest of us were supposed to chant in unison: "We welcome you, oh Ed, to the Community of Hronir."

When Ed sat down, the circle would reform, and soon Plammer would place her hands on another head, moaning, "Your Dlønic name emerges from the great sea. Rise to accept it, Ted."

"We welcome you, oh Ted, to the Community of Hronir!"

The names were all monosyllabic words that rhymed with Ed. Some of them were real names. After descending into the great sea, Plammer emerged with the names Red, Jed, and Ned. Others were words that I'd never heard anyone use as names. Wed, Bread, and Led. Still others were nonsense. Plammer named one clown Pted and another Zed. After naming half of the clowns, however, she seemed to get confused. Her voice squeaked more often and she started repeating herself. When Petey became the fourth Ed, I spoke up.

"You seem to be getting confused," I said. "Wouldn't it be simpler if you just went in alphabetical order?"

"Certainly not," Plammer squeaked. "What an absurd outside idea."

"Well, I just thought," I said, "it would help you to keep track. Since you already have four Eds, I, for example, wouldn't want to be called Ed."

"Hush," Plammer murmured. "I feel your name coming." She ran to me and grabbed my head. Squeezing my temples with her forefingers, she proclaimed, "You are Bed."

"Bed? That's a stupid name. I don't want to be called Bed. How about Haunted or Wasted?""

Plammer shook her head. She looked like she was about to cry.

"Rotted, Hated, or Hamstead," I said. "I'd even accept Worsted."

"Well," she squeaked. Her voice was going to pieces, as if she'd been made to play a part written for trombone. "How about Fred? We don't have a Fred in class yet."

"I like Worsted," I said. "Why don't you call me Worsted?"

"It might be confusing. I mean, it seems a bit long." Plammer shook her head as if she was afraid to pass judgment on the matter. Probably no one had ever questioned the naming ritual before. "I would have to ask Dr. Rabbit about that."

"Who is Dr. Rabbit?"

"The head," she hesitated. "I mean the Hron among Hronir."

"The one with the green hair?"

She bit her lip and nodded.

"Forget it," I mumbled. "I'll be your Fred."

"Oh, that's wonderful," she said, clapping her hands. "Your Dlønic name emerges from the great sea. Rise to accept it, Fred."

As I stood up, the rest of the clowns chanted: "We welcome you, oh Fred, to the Community of Hronir."

After the renaming was finished, Plammer passed out little mirrors so that we could admire ourselves. We were made to sit with a partner and describe what we saw in the mirror. When we'd finished examining ourselves, we were supposed to name at least three things that we liked before passing the mirror to our partners who would then do the same thing.

I was paired with Ed, the former Petey. Looking in the mirror, he giggled and said that he liked his blue wig, the purple diamond under his left eye, and the rubber ball on the end of his nose. He did not mention any of his own features. Even though he's an idiot, he's not entirely ugly. He has nice green eyes and big pouty lips that you wouldn't mind kissing if they belonged to someone else.

When my turn came to look in the mirror, I couldn't help but sneak a glance at Plammer. She had resumed her lotus position at the center of the room. With her mouth shut, she looked magnificent. I pictured her rescuing someone from a tsunami, her ample cleavage lurching from a bright orange Baywatch bathing suit. I took her beauty as a personal affront—an attack on flat-chested, big-nosed me. And I decided to find something to like about myself.

I told Ed that I liked my nose. I liked it because it was bigger than anyone else's in the room. Indeed, it was so big that the rubber ball barely fit. I said that he wouldn't have recognized me if it hadn't been for my nose. Then, I noticed that if I pulled my hair back I could see my own olive brown skin up under the roots. Next to the pasty white greasepaint, it had this undulating sheen, the quicksilver temerity of living things. I liked my odd, vibrant color. It was mine. Finally, I said that I liked my eyes, and that was no lie. I don't think I give up anything to Plammer in that department. My eyes are shaped like a mandorla, the illuminated, almond center in certain paintings of the body of Christ; my pupils are a brown liqueur in a slanting, Byzantine frame. My eyes, in fact, are just like Lola's. Looking into the mirror was like having generations of my family staring back at me. I remembered how my great-great-grandmother had escaped from the American soldiers, and I felt proud. I felt that Plammer was a nobody, a nothing, beside my vital eyes. I told Ed that my eyes were what I liked best.

It didn't matter what I said to Ed, he just giggled like an idiot and called me ugly. But as long as he kept his fingers out of his nose, I didn't really care.

When we were done with the mirrors, we formed a circle again to share what we had learned; only instead of talking about ourselves, we were supposed to tell what we liked about our partners. Everyone said that they liked their partner's wig and greasepaint. Plammer kept nodding her head and squeaking words of encouragement. When it was Ed's turn, he said what everyone else had said. He admired my wig and my greasepaint.

I wasn't about to admire Ed's wig, but I also wasn't going to tell the truth. "I don't like anything about Ed," I said. "He's mean, he's stupid, and he picks his nose in front of other people."

Ed just giggled, but I think I finally got to Plammer. "Children," she said, "who remembers the third tenet of the Community of Hronir?"

Hands flew up like frightened birds.

Then, at Plammer's prompting, the clowns recited in unison. "All students, teachers, and administrators of the Community, Hronir like yourself, always do the best they can. This is a truth I keep in my heart."

I didn't say anything. There was no point in arguing with a room full of idiots.

Plammer stroked my cheek with her long red fingernails. "We know you didn't mean what you said," she said. But though she spoke softly, it felt more like she was threatening me rather than comforting me. "We've all been damaged by the outside. But by working together we can free ourselves. We are here to transform you, to liberate you. You all remember Dr. Rabbit's fourth rule."

This time, she didn't have to prompt them. The recitation went on of its own accord: "A Hron is free to question anything that has been learned on the outside. A Hron is free to speak out about mistakes, personal failings, problems and shortcomings."

The next ritual reminded me of confession, or more precisely, of one of those talk shows that specializes in women who love their daughters' lovers, sons of hookers who hate their fathers, polygamists who fantasize about animals, and boys who sleep with their mothers' golf partners. As we went around the circle, we were each supposed to describe some event from our lives on the outside that demonstrated how we had been warped. All of the clowns seemed anxious to have a turn at wailing and whimpering. They whined and thumped themselves, and blubbered through their snouts as if in spasms. A little boy with big ears went on and on about his bathroom habits. One girl told about a boyfriend who used to beat her up. "Do you thank me much?" he'd asked her one day. And she'd replied, "Beyond all measure."

When my turn came, I felt sick to my stomach. I thought about tearing off my headgear and giving up on Bri and my stupid adventure. Why should I share anything with these fools? I couldn't see how taking part in this farce would get me closer to achieving my goals. The only thing it could do was to turn me into one of them.

"You can take a while to think about it, Fred," Plammer said. "What do you regret?"

"The only thing I regret," I said, "is that you're turning me into a clown."

This was too much for the lovely Ms. Plammer. Her face slid into her hands the way an egg slides from a well-greased pan. Underneath she wore a strange wooden mask, with ghoulish red eyes, green fuzzy eyebrows, and the fangs of a rakshasa. As she struggled to put her face back on, she screeched at me, "Don't ever say that word! Don't ever say that word!"

Soon, the other clowns were on their feet screaming, pounding their chests, and waving their hands in my face. I couldn't understand a word they were saying, but I noticed that Petey did not join in the fun. He was too busy picking his nose and pouting with his cute plump lips.

"Clowns!" I taunted. "Clowns, clowns, clowns."

I thought that Plammer was going to hit me, but she did something much more effective instead. On her belt she wore a device that I'm sure every teacher dreams of owning. It was the size and shape of a garage door-opener. Once she'd gotten her face back on, she aimed at me and fired. I went blind for a moment, felt a tingling in my spine, and suddenly I was sitting in an office in front of a huge desk.

CHAPTER NINETEEN

The desk was so big that I could not see over or around it. As far as I could tell, it filled the room except for the narrow space where I was sitting. I could hear muffled voices that seemed to come from nearby, but I did not have the feeling that anyone else was in the room with me.

Even though it was stupid, I started feeling the way I feel every time I get into trouble. I felt heavy and a little bit sick to my stomach. I thought that maybe I shouldn't have argued with Plammer. She was probably just doing her job. I wondered what my parents would think when they found out I'd screwed up again. Then I remembered where I was, that it was all just a part of this stupid game.

After a while, when I started to get bored, I kicked the desk to see if it was solid. I heard a rustling as if I'd disturbed a giant rat or ferret who'd made its nest amid the papers inside the desk. Realizing that the thing I had disturbed might try to attack me, I decided to climb up onto the desk where I would at least have a chance to see it first.

I had to jump from the chair to reach the top of the desk, but then it was easy to pull myself up. The sight that greeted me on top of the desk, however, almost made me lose my balance and fall back down again. Sticking out of the surface of the desk were three sets of legs. Apparently, the bodies to which they belonged were inside the desk. They reminded me of kids doing handstands underwater, trying to keep their legs straight above the surface. Only, these legs were fully clothed. All three sets wore pleated, freshly pressed suit pants, not to mention black wing tips, expertly polished and buffed. The only way to tell them apart was the socks. The one on my left wore black socks with crimson paisleys that reminded me of Emily. The one in the middle wore beautiful blue woolen socks that barely covered the ankles, so that each time the legs moved a patch of thick black hair showed between the cuff of the pants and the ridge of the socks. The one to the right had solved this problem by attaching garters to his pair of pea-green polyester socks.

I could hear the same voices that I'd heard before, only now they were much clearer. Apparently the owners of the legs were talking inside the desk.

"Okay," said Pea-green. "How do you get from France to God in seven?"

"Easy," shouted Blue. "First you change the channel."

Paisley snorted. "And the Channel separates England from France."

"Excuse me," I said.

It seemed they couldn't hear me.

"And France is where they make the finest pants," sang Blue.

"Which hang elegantly below your shoes," Paisley proclaimed.

"Which in turn contain your socks," observed Blue.

Now there was a pause.

"Excuse me," I tried again.

"If you've been sent here, I'm certain that there's no excuse." Pea-green's legs writhed as if someone had tickled him or lit a fire on the soles of his feet.

"Who are you?" I said.

"We are the Committee," announced Pea-green.

"Formerly known as the Board," added Blue.

"What are you doing?" I said.

"Strictly speaking, we are not doing anything," said Paisley. "We are in charge."

"But just now," I said, "you were talking about something."

"We're creating a document," Paisley shouted, whipping his legs like a Thai kick-boxer and grazing my jaw with the smooth leather on the sole of his shoe.

As I was stepping back carefully, trying to make sure that I didn't fall off the desk or move into the range of one of the others, Blue began convulsing Elvis-style.

"We're crafting a statement," he said.

"An educational vision," added the still writhing Pea-green.

"You might call us theorists," said Paisley. "We're devising a revolutionary new theory."

"It sounded to me like you were playing a game," I said. "And I got the impression you were stumped. So I thought, if you liked, I might be able to help you."

The legs went limp for a moment. There was a sound of papers rustling, but none of the committee members spoke.

Suddenly Paisley whipped around in another deadly manoeuvre and shouted, "Well, let us have it."

"First you have to promise that you'll help me."

"Of course," said Pea-green, straightening momentarily. "That's what we're here for."

"Come on then," growled Blue. "We haven't got all day. We're busy men."

"Well, socks are holey," I said. "And we've been taught that God is the holiest of all."

"No, no, no." Pea-green began to writhe again. "That won't do."

I ducked to avoid his foot and edged closer to Blue, who, unfortunately, began convulsing again at that very moment. Catching me in the crook of his knee, he sent me sprawling to the edge of the desk.

"Socks love fresh air," Blue proclaimed.

"And that, like God, is neither here nor there," howled Paisley.

"Do you see?" Pea-green proclaimed. "The business of education is no trifling matter."

I had no idea what the legs were talking about, but I had no one else to talk to. "I don't understand who you are or what any of this has to do with anything else. I don't know why I'm here. I can't even figure out what you're trying to teach me."

"Teach?" Paisley took a swipe at thin air, and I heard the vertebrae cracking in his back. "We're not teaching. We're educating."

"Transforming," gurgled Blue.

"Liberating," sighed Pea-green, letting his legs dangle so his toes touched the table top.

"What are you liberating me from?"

"From stifling societal limits, from the outside, from yourself."

"What if I don't want to be liberated?"

Now Blue's convulsions became worse than ever. "All Hronir seek liberation," he shouted. "You are a Hron. Therefore you seek liberation."

"What makes you think that I'm a Hron?" I said. "I never told anyone that I wanted to be a Hron. You decided that yourselves. I just want to find my friend and get out of here."

Blue's legs slowed to a quiver, and his voice changed pitch accordingly. Where before he'd tried to bully me, now it seemed he wanted to coax me. "I know that you are a Hron because I can picture your education. I can see you being transformed, becoming one with the community."

Now the three began to chant in unison: "All Hronir have been made members of the community. You have been made a member of the community. Therefore, you are a Hron."

"That doesn't follow necessarily," I said. "What if I don't accept the tenets?"

"That would be against the tenets."

All of this was nonsense. I remembered that Fra Umberto had told me at the beginning of the voyage to brace myself with reason. "You're begging the question," I said.

"You're applying outside logic," said Pea-green.

In the heat of the argument, I'd forgotten to keep clear of the legs. Now it was Blue who caught me in a scissor lock.

"Now remember," he said, squeezing the air out of my lungs. "All outsiders are liars. Outside logic was invented by outsiders. Therefore, outside logic lies."

"I'm an outsider," I grunted. "I'm just passing through."

Blue tightened his legs. "No, you're not."

"I'm a liar," I added.

"You're lying."

"That's my point," I said, digging my fingernails into one of his hairy legs.

He howled and released me. I collapsed on the floor, feeling hollow and sick, as if something inside of me had been broken. I tried to stand up, but I still couldn't breathe.

"You are morons. All three of you, all six of you, or whatever," I grunted, pulling myself up to my feet. "In fact, it wouldn't surprise me if you're all just bits of the one big moron that lives inside the desk."

"That's enough," shouted Paisley. "Run along to class now." But there was nowhere for me to run, no way to duck as he wound up and kicked me so hard I flew through the wall of the office.

CHAPTER TWENTY

The hallway was filled with clowns in whiteface hurrying to get to their classes. For a while I just stood and watched them, trying to see if I could pick out Bri. One clown looked promising. He was the right height, and I thought I saw a trace of a mole peeking through the greasepaint on the left side of his nose. I decided to follow him.

He even walked like Bri, taking short, quick steps and keeping his arms extended stiffly at his sides. Though he didn't say anything, I thought he recognized me too. Maybe he was afraid to let me know. I couldn't decide whether I should speak. I wanted to reach over and hold his hand. But my recent experiences in Dløn had made me wary.

I followed him to class but stopped short in the doorway. The room was full of pianos, and a clown was seated at each of them banging out the opening bars of *"Für Elise."* At the front of the class, pointing at the notes on a giant screen was Mrs. Quinn, my first piano teacher. I had put up with a lot in Dløn, but this was just too cruel. Mrs. Quinn had the ability to make even Bach seem boring.

Bri sat down at one of the pianos and began to play. I thought about doing the same, but I was afraid of getting stuck in this class. With my hand on the doorknob, I called his name. "Bri," I shouted. "Brian Bållerup, is that you?"

No one looked up. They just kept hammering on the keys. The sound was maddening. I don't know why I'd expected a response. Even if the clown was Bri, I had no real reason to believe that he wanted me to find him. Maybe he was trying to avoid me. Maybe he was just messing around with me. Maybe this whole adventure was his idea of a joke— a way of getting back at me. It wouldn't be the first time that I'd met someone who was nice in real life but turned out to be a total jerk in virtual reality.

When they reached the repeat, I ran back out into the hall. If it had been Bri, he would've looked up at least. I decided it wasn't him. It was just another illusion, sucking me deeper and deeper into Dløn. For a moment, I was furious. I wanted to go back and attack him, slam the keycover down on his fingers. But I knew that wouldn't get me anywhere. You couldn't confront anything head-on in Dløn.

Everyone was in class now. The hall was so quiet I could hear the blood rushing in my ears: it roared like a typhoon. I walked up and down the hall, almost hoping that someone would find me and tell me where I was supposed to go or harass me about not being there.

Where before I had thought that Dløn had something to do with me—even that I was partly responsible for its existence—now it seemed to have some terrible and inscrutable purpose of its own. Standing in the empty hall reminded me of lurking in certain mainframes: I could get in and watch what was going on, but I couldn't possibly hope to grasp what it meant.

I walked up and down the length of the hall several times, trying to figure out what to do next. Maybe the real Bri was in one of the rooms waiting to be found. Maybe Bri was nowhere to be found. Maybe this had nothing to do with Bri or with me. Maybe Fra Umberto was right. Dløn was a puzzle. To solve it, you had to remain patient, stay in the process. Eventually, the pattern would become clear. The pieces would start to fit together.

After a while I decided to open doors at random. What could possibly happen to me that hadn't already happened?

In the first room, a man was drawing a picture on the floor. It was a picture of a fish or a whale—I couldn't tell which because there were no specific details. There were no gills but there was also no blow-hole. The fish was smiling and its eye was much too big. If the fish had been an egg, the eye would have been its yoke: that's how big it was.

I asked the man what kind of fish it was.

"It is not a fish," he said.

"A whale?"

"A decoration," he said. And he continued his work.

A group of Hronir, presumably his students, sat on the floor in another part of the room, whispering and playing with each other's hair. They did not seem the least bit interested in his drawing or in our discussion. They did not seem the least bit interested in me either. When I smiled at them, they stopped talking and looked away.

The next few classes that I visited had this same feeling. No one seemed to care whether I came or went. No one seemed to care about what was going on in the classes. No one argued. No one raised her voice. The rooms were all very neat and clean. There were no messes in the rooms. Nothing was accidental.

In one room things were different. The Hronir, seated in groups of four around little tables with video monitors embedded in them, were making all manner of strange noises. I walked over to one of the tables and stood behind the clowns. No one seemed to mind, not even the teacher who was pacing the floor, moving between the desks slowly, methodically, as if he were tracing a pattern.

The video monitor displayed a series of simple math problems. In order to solve them, you had only to keep in mind the order of operations. In each case, the equations could be reduced to the same simple operation: $3 + 1$. It took me less than a minute to solve them all in my head.

But for the clowns sitting at the closest table and else-where in the classroom, the equations seemed to inspire an entirely different set of operations. They clapped their hands and nodded to each other. They grunted like animals. They howled. They coughed, whistled, and scratched their arm-pits. But, they did not leave their seats or take their eyes from the screens.

Meanwhile, the teacher continued to pace, calmly, as if the clowns were doing precisely what he expected them to do. As I watched and listened, I thought I noticed a pattern to the gestures and animal noises. It seemed as if the groups were following a musical score, as if the equations on the screen contained secret instructions. I did not have the sense that the clowns enjoyed what they were doing. Beneath the greasepaint, their faces showed no signs of emotion at all. Something about the way they looked at the screens, with their pupils dilated, gave me the sense that they didn't know what they were doing or why they were doing it.

Eventually the teacher's path brought him face to face with me. He was a tall man with thinning hair and nervous gray eyes. He seemed more uncomfortable than anyone I had ever met in Dløn, as if he knew that what he was doing was wrong, or at least suspected it. If I hadn't spoken to him, I think he would have pretended that I wasn't there and walked past me. I've noticed that when adults are ashamed of what they're doing, they try to avoid discussing it with children.

I grabbed him by the arm, so he had to stop and look at me. "The answer is four," I said.

When he looked at me, I realized that I'd made a mis-take. His mouth dropped, and his eyes became a pair of great gray egg yolks, as big as those of the decorative fish. He wheezed several times, as if gathering the strength to scream, but nothing came of it. Now the Hronir abandoned their rituals. Instead of watching the monitors, they stared at us.

When it became clear that the teacher wasn't going to address me, one of the Hronir who'd been sitting at the nearest table stood up suddenly. "Everything learned outside is false, destructive, and evil," he shouted.

Now the other Hronir stood up, and soon they were all pounding on their tables and shouting together: "Every Hron always has fun. If it's not fun, we don't do it in Dløn! All Hronir always do the best they can! A Hron is free to question anything that has been learned on the outside. A Hron must not question any of these precious tenets, for they are the foundation of our community. Without them, our community, our family, will not function."

As they shouted, they moved towards us. Soon we were encircled by angry clowns. I thought I recognized one of the Eds from Plammer's class, but I wasn't sure. They all looked insane, frenzied, as if they were ready to tear us apart.

As it turned out, they didn't care about me. It was only the teacher who interested them. The first Hron who got hold of him ripped his head right off his shoulders. It came off easily like a baby doll's head. There was no blood and no sound of bones breaking. In fact, it was only when his head had been separated from his shoulders that the teacher regained the ability to speak.

"Think about what you're doing," I heard him cry.

But soon the other Hronir attacked his body, which, surprisingly, had not fallen over. The body, it turned out, was filled with straw. Still reciting the four tenets, the Hronir pulled out big handfuls of the teacher's straw and threw it up in the air until there was nothing left of the body but an empty pair of pants and a button-down collared shirt. Grasping the teacher's hair, the first Hron spun the head around lasso-style and launched it at the far wall of the classroom.

The head seemed to fly in slow motion. The Hronir watched impassively until it landed with a dull thud on the floor. Then pandemonium broke loose. In a flurry of rustling nylon, they ran towards the head, pushing each other out of the the way, trying to be the first to get hold of it. Their shouts and cries no longer followed a pattern. They forgot the tenets. This process was new, crude, electric.

The first clown who picked up the head was bitten and dropped it. The next was wise enough to hold onto the hair, but he was tackled by five or six others. Soon, it was huckle-smuckle, rumble-stumble spilling out into the hallway. One clown would get his hands on the head and hang onto it for as long as he could. Then, right before he was tackled, he would launch it, and the others would dive and try to get hold of it.

I followed the crowd. Everyone was frantic, crazy, out of control. After a moment, the bell rang and the hall filled up with Hronir from all of the classrooms. Now, it was wall-to-wall clowns, everybody pushing and bumping. Everyone excited, frightened, edgy. There wasn't an adult anywhere in sight. I wondered where Rabbit was. Where were the teachers? It occurred to me that maybe they were hiding.

With every passing moment, the crowd seemed to grow more dangerous, more powerful. They elbowed and shoved. They grabbed, they twitched, they pinched. They kicked and punched lockers. When one locker flew open, they shoved the miserable teacher's head in and closed it up again.

Once, when a clown fell down, several others surrounded him and began to kick him. They kicked him in the ribs. They kicked him in the groin. And when he reached down to protect himself, they kicked him in the face. The kick to the face made a strange brittle sound, as if he'd been chewing a mouthful of corn chips. I saw blood dripping from his mouth and onto his outfit. I wanted to go and help him, but then the crowd surged forward and there was nothing to do. I moved with it, afraid of getting trampled myself. I wondered if this was the kind of community Rabbit and Plammer were hoping to create.

For some mysterious reason, I began to recognize faces through the greasepaint. I saw Margot Butte, mastermind of the most evil clique in the fifth grade and editor-in-chief of a dozen slam books including one about me entitled, *"Chicken Catch-a-Greenbitch."* She gave it to me as a going-away present, all wrapped up with a bow and everything. Every page had an obscene drawing of me on it. There were jokes about my clothes, about my family name, about my hairstyle, about my nose, even about things that I thought I'd told my friends in confidence.

I had to scratch Ron Sliff's cheek to keep him from rubbing against me and grabbing my behind. I looked away when I recognized Stefano Turblocco from Trieste who'd made a small fortune taking bets on the fights he organized in the playground. He especially enjoyed collecting the winnings when I beat up boys. Each kid I looked at, I recognized. It seemed that every beast I'd ever known was there in that hallway, going in the same direction, rushing onwards, a mob of cruel, sickening, foul children. And I was one of them.

CHAPTER TWENTY-ONE

Durian is the oldest fruit in the world. Dinosaurs ate it. The smell and the color of the flesh attracted them. The earliest durian had red flesh. The dinosaurs ate dozens at a time, swallowing everything, including the seeds. Endosaurochory —that's the scientific term for plants that rely on the intestines of reptiles for dispersal.

If it were up to me, I would eat like a dinosaur. I would eat only rice, nuts, and fruits, mostly durian. I would wander about, eating only when I felt hungry. I wouldn't eat with other people. I would keep to myself.

I've always thought that cafeterias were designed to promote eating disorders. Who wants to eat a ball of mashed potatoes molded in a plastic glove? Who wants to sit in a room where three hundred other people are slurping, crunching, swallowing, sucking, belching, talking, masticating openmouthed the same pulpy potato muck. They might as well pour the slop in a trough and let you bury your face to the eyes like they do in the Community of Hronir mess hall.

Don't ask me how I got there. I was buoyed by the crowd through a long dimly lit hallway, down a half-dozen flights of stairs and out into a glassed-in courtyard with a view of the atrium and its nonsensical alphabet soup. I looked for a means of escape but found none: the walls being made of the same impenetrable substance as the mermaids' tanks. Pushed through a set of bright green sliding doors, I found myself wedged between two of the Eds from Plammer's class, who would have been skin-diving in the muck, I'm sure, if only they'd brought their snorkels.

The trough was mounted on a table. It was about ten centimeters deep, two meters across and ten meters long. Clowns sat on either side of the table, packed in shoulder to shoulder—a good sixty or seventy swilling from our trough. The trough seemed to have a narcotic effect on the Hronir. Listening to them chomping and slurping, you would never have guessed that they'd been rioting just a few minutes before.

Every few minutes one of several muscular women dressed in orange jumpsuits would come by to dump more slops in the trough or to shove a reluctant face into the muck. Fortunately, I caught onto the game right away: they didn't really care if you were eating as long as you kept your face down close to the swill and made it look like you were hard at work.

I suppose that a pig would've been thrilled with the pickings, but I've never put my face closer to anything more sickening. Of course, there were some things that by themselves wouldn't have been all that bad to eat. I saw a slice of sour dough bread, homemade potato gnocchi, rice cakes of all sorts including my favorite three-egg bibingka, an open-faced Danish liverwurst sandwich with a cucumber garnish, matzo balls, wontons, chicken pandan, shad roe timbales with onion and cucumber sauce, a sweet potato and pineapple soufflé, a Pop-Tart, a slice of black forest cake, three or four macaroons, two butter thins, and an almond croissant.

The problem was the soup: all of these interesting tidbits were floating in a broth of raspberry jello, chicken soup, spaghetti sauce, chocolate milk, vinegar, seaweed, rice (tons and tons of rice), half-chewed hot-dog bits, potato peels, tomato and banana ketchup, soy sauce, Worcestershire sauce, oyster sauce, Coke, breakfast cereal, yogurt (plain and with fruit, low-fat and no-fat), orange juice, coffee grounds, and grated cheese in every shade from egg-yolk to olive.

I was trying to think of a way to escape from the table when the head of a snake poked through the surface of the slop not two inches from my nose. It was a tiny snake head, no bigger than the tip of my little finger, perfectly carved like a piece of jade.

"What are you doing there?" I asked the snake.

It licked the air with its beautiful tongue, a hair-like filament of silver wire.

"Do you know a way to get out of here?"

The snake seemed to ponder my question before diving back into the muck and slithering away.

"Hey!" The Ed on my left grabbed my arm and shook me.

I looked at him. His face was covered with gruel and he had a candied yam dangling from his ear in the place of a lobe.

"Were you talking to a stinkin' snake?" said the Ed, still hanging onto my arm, squeezing so hard it hurt.

Apparently all of the Hronic lessons about community and understanding had been lost on this Ed.

"What's wrong with talking to a snake?" I said.

"The only thing a snake will do is bite you, if you don't bite him first." Ed chuckled then dunked his head back in the trough.

This time it was my turn to grab hold of him. I took him by the hair on the very top of his head, the only part that was not drenched completely in waste. I pulled, and his wig came off. He surfaced, swinging and clutching at me, trying to get back the wig even before he could see what I'd done with it. "Give it back! Give it back!" he gurgled, dribbling slop, the little green snake head sticking out from the corner of his mouth.

"If you tell me how to get out of here," I said, holding the wig behind my back so he couldn't reach it.

"I don't know," he said.

"Fine," I said. "Then I won't give you back the wig."

"You'll never get out of here," whispered the snake.

Ed sucked the snake into his mouth and crunched it.

"You're disgusting," I said.

He wrinkled his nose and squinted at me. His eyes were pinkish, like the crew-cut scalp under his wig. "All right," he said, pausing to chew on the snake, his cud, whatever else he had in his mouth. "I'll tell you how to get out, but first you have to give me my hair."

"Do you think I'm stupid?" I said. "Tell me first."

He sighed. "I'll tell you, but only if you tell me what you're doing here—how you got here, all that."

"Why should I tell you?"

"I'm your big brother," he said. "I'm going to take care of you."

He sounded sincere, and I was tired. Fra Umberto would have told me not to waste my sympathy on characters. But Fra Umberto was a character himself. Ed seemed to be a player.

Sometimes I make stupid mistakes. Sometimes I'm just too trusting. I told Ed about my search for Bri. I didn't tell him about all the places I'd been, but I did tell him about the Barbies, my grandfather the rat, the *tikbalang,* the soldiers, the gargoyles—all the stuff that a boy would be interested in. When I was done, he wanted to see the picture of Bri.

"Let me see. Let me see the picture," he kept saying.

Some kids want your stuff because they can use it. Some kids are just plain greedy. But Ed was the kind of kid who steals stuff just because it's valuable to you. That kind of thief doesn't care about stuff. He's only interested in getting power over you, making you do things you don't want to do, humiliating, or hurting you. That kind of thief is the worst kind.

It's true that I had stolen from him first, but I never had the intention of keeping his wig. Now you might argue that Ed didn't know that. But Ed was much bigger and stronger than I am; he could have taken the wig back any time he wanted. Looking back, I realize that Ed had played along with me because he'd been thinking the whole time that he could get something out of the game.

That something was Bri's picture. As soon as I showed it to him, he grabbed it and threw it like a frisbee to a kid at the other end of the trough. That kid threw it to another one, who threw it to another, who ripped it up and stirred it into the slop. I tried to chase the picture, but two orange ladies grabbed me faster than you can say "The Fat King Fergus" and dumped me head first into the trough.

CHAPTER TWENTY-TWO

I'm sure I would have drowned if Fra Umberto hadn't come to my rescue again. He grabbed hold of my heels and yanked me out of the slop. After pounding my back with his fist, so I choked up the chunks I'd swallowed, he stood me back on my feet.

I wanted to give him a hug, but he seemed to be in a hurry.

"*Su andiamo!* Let's go!" he said, grabbing my hand and breaking into a run, his eyebrows twitching a delightful polka. Though I was growing tired of these last-minute interventions, I was happy to follow him.

In the meantime, chaos had broken out in the mess hall. Clowns were leaping into the muck, wrestling with the orange-clad ladies, dumping the troughs onto the floor, hurling great chunks of bread and fistfuls of bean curd through the air.

We moved through the crowd quickly, guarded on all sides by a phalanx of the biggest, most ridiculous soldiers I've ever seen. They were dressed like rejects from the Mod Squad or Russian sailors at a disco. They wore polyester shirts unbuttoned to the navel, fake gold chains around their necks and collars like the wings of the SST. Their pants were checkered, hip-hugging bell-bottoms with flares the size of elephant feet, and though they were already at least seven feet tall they tottered like windmills on three-inch platform shoes. Finally, to crown their glory, they wore plastic, children's Viking hats atop their David Cassidy locks, held in place with elastic bands that carved deep grooves into the flesh beneath their chins.

They were armed with yellow wiffle ball bats which they wielded with amazing accuracy and power, swatting anyone who came into range, toppling clowns and lunch ladies alike.

Their leader, a woman, was dressed in an even more entrancing outfit. Under a black fishnet shawl, she wore a skintight jumpsuit of sparkling red spandex. Dangling around her neck in what would have been her cleavage if she'd had breasts was a three-inch iron cross. In place of a Viking hat she wore a tin tiara with glass rubies the size of cherries. Her hair was a mess of Farrah Fawcett curls. A pair of fringed, black high-heeled boots encased her legs to the thighs. Instead of a wiffle ball bat, she wielded a riding crop in her right hand which she snapped periodically at nothing, as if she were battling to control a skittish, invisible horse.

As we moved towards the exit, she shouted orders to the Vikings: "Hark and hasten fellows! Trundle yonder coxcomb. Sly as an ox, he lingers, up to his cheeks in the fat of windy hopes. By troth, I'll have you whipt, as my name is Malacoda—to't boys!"

Although the Vikings lumbered through the crowd, wobbling knock-kneed like virgin skaters afraid of kissing the pavement, we did finally make it to the door and out onto a grated platform, dangling above a dark, gaping pit.

It wasn't until the last of the Vikings had slammed the door behind him and stood gasping for breath on the platform that I gathered the courage to look down. We were in a sort of shaft. Hundreds of meters below, there was a patch of white floor, strangely illuminated, undulating, as if it were covered with steam or hyperactive ants. As my eyes adjusted I began to distinguish the things around us. Everything was rough and unfinished. It looked like we were in an engine room, the guts of the machine. I could see the heavy metal girders that supported the ceiling and walls, the huge metal bolts that held them in place.

I noticed that Fra Umberto was still holding my hand. I gave him a squeeze to signal that he could let go, but he must have thought I wanted to talk.

"Not now," he mumbled in Italian. His voice had an unfamiliar edge to it, almost as if he were nervous. "Follow the Vikings."

At the end of the platform, a catwalk stretched out into the darkness. The catwalk was about a meter wide, and there was a network of pipes running overhead. There was no way the Vikings would be able to walk across. The Vikings grunted at each other and shook their bats in the direction of the catwalk. It was obvious that none of them wanted to go first.

After this had gone on for several minutes, the woman, Malacoda, losing her patience, cracked her crop across the nearest set of Viking buttocks and began to rant again. "Marry, seize thine innards," she shouted, "or I shall bring to bear upon thy pates the most unrepentant stench of this, my fetid humor. Tarry not, I prithee, or thy eruptions shall be breached."

The threat had an immediate effect on the Vikings. The one closest to the catwalk got down on hands and knees and began to crawl out into the darkness. When half a dozen of them had gone, the ones standing beside us indicated with little shoves that we were to go next.

Fra Umberto let go of my hand. "You go ahead," he said. "I will come right behind you. If you start to fall, I'll be there."

There was no need for me to crawl. It was like walking on a sidewalk. The pipes loomed in the darkness above my head. By ducking their heads slightly to the side, even Fra Umberto and Malacoda could walk quite comfortably. When I noticed that she stayed right behind him, I got the sense that he really was their hostage. I wondered how it had happened and what it meant. If he was, as he'd said, the librarian from Apeiron snooping around Dløn, he was in deep trouble. Most environments treated characters from other environments like viruses: they killed them. I hoped that he was just pretending to be captured or that this was just another Dlønic illusion. More than anything, I didn't want him to get hurt.

I kept hoping that Fra Umberto would grab my hand and lead me down another catwalk that the Vikings and Malacoda hadn't noticed. I kept hoping that he would at least say something reassuring, that he would whisper in Italian. "Things aren't what they seem. *Forza! Coraggio!*" But his breathing was heavy and his footfalls sounded unsteady.

It seemed strange that a bunch of idiots could gain control over someone as brilliant as Fra Umberto. Then I remembered the picture I'd lost to the fools at the trough. I wasn't all that disturbed about having lost it. I knew what Bri looked like. But who's to say that Bri would look like Bri in Dløn? He might have disguised himself, or he might not have been there at all. Anyway, at the moment, I wasn't all that interested in finding him. I was much more interested in finding out what was going on. I wanted to understand the mess that Fra Umberto and I had gotten ourselves into. I needed to know if there was any way out.

CHAPTER TWENTY-THREE

When we reached another platform at the end of the cat-walk, I grabbed Fra Umberto's hand and leaped at the space beneath the railing. But the priest made no move to follow, and his fingers slipped from mine. With surprising agility, two Vikings moved to block my way. Bending over, they took hold of my arms, one apiece, and lifted me off the ground. I struggled and kicked, but it was useless. Holding me up like a stuffed bear or a baby doll, they bowed ever so slightly in the direction of Malacoda.

Now Fra Umberto tried to help me. "Let her go!" he growled, his eyebrows twitching as if trying to free them-selves from his face. But no sooner had he taken a step to-wards me than four of the giants grabbed him and threw him to the floor.

Moving with an exaggerated sway of the hips, struggling like a man pretending to be a woman, Malacoda approached me. When she was right in front of me, her toes touching mine, she grabbed my cheeks and squeezed them like they were bread dough. For a while she said nothing, and I thought I could hear the distant hum of an engine deep in the pit. Her eyes were that bright hue of purple that can only be bought in a store. After examining my face, she readjusted her hold, pinching my nose so I had to open my mouth to breathe, and began ranting again in her strange, indecipher-able palaver, "How comes it hence, unwing'd varlet, that thou in want of pruning seekest succor in contempt and then possessed of failure, drowning, reacheth forth and drowneth no less softly?"

After her tirade, Malacoda grimaced and sucked on her teeth, great jagged yellow monuments with black cracks in the enamel. I had no idea what she was talking about, but it occurred to me that the missing lines from Fra Umberto's books had somehow wound up in her mangling jaws.

"Excuse me," I said, trying to speak as clearly as possible through her grasping fingers, "but I couldn't understand a word you said."

"Mistress Malacoda is known throughout Dløn for her erudition," Fra Umberto muttered, his eyebrows forming a single, ironic arch that spanned his brow.

"I still don't understand what she said."

"She said you're in trouble."

"What sort of trouble?"

"Big trouble."

Malacoda readjusted her grip on my face, inserting a sharp green nail into my right nostril, then she kicked Fra Umberto in the groin. He grunted and twisted away from her foot.

"Wouldst or wouldst not," she squawked. "If thou couldst but dismember, and in the 'membering make whole again, thou mightst still be thought most right and just, for is it not nobler in failing to vouchsafe what one might, to act boldly, and in so doing to harbor no ill regrets?—Nay, and fie upon it. I shall have you flayed for such outbursts!"

I wanted to kill her, or at least to spit in her face, but I knew that it was not a good idea. Fra Umberto was still sprawled on the ground, moaning as if Malacoda had really hurt him. I remembered the way Fra Umberto had handled me the first time we'd met in Apeiron. I wondered what trick she'd used to give him substance. I hoped that he was pretending, using Malacoda to lead us somewhere. I hoped that he was on the verge of solving the puzzle. I told myself that he was planning a trap, that he was going to fry Malacoda along with the rest of the assholes who inhabited Dløn. The other possibilities were just too depressing to think about.

When I did not answer Malacoda, she released my face, muttering more erudite phrases under her breath. Then she gave a signal to one of the Vikings, and he opened a door that led from the landing into a dark, cavernous room.

CHAPTER TWENTY-FOUR

It took me a while to get a sense of the room. Although it was empty except for our group, it smelled of crowds—a mixture of sweat, perfume, and shoe polish. In the middle of the room a big, old, mirror ball was spinning, casting geometrical swatches of colored light onto the floor, the walls, the Vikings' faces.

When the music started (a disco hit from my parents' childhood), a dozen of the Vikings formed a line and began dancing. The dance was intricate, with all sorts of turns and dips, shuffles and twists. They danced in time, but they danced without passion. They looked at their feet, and they leaned forward like herons hunting for fish, or like embarrassed jockeys. The effect was hilarious, but for some reason, I felt sorry for them. There was something so pathetic about the performance and their costumes.

I've only been to two or three dances in my life, and I have never danced with a boy. I've never even been asked to dance. Once I tried asking a boy to dance with me. His sneakers squeaked on the gym floor as he ran away. Diving into a group of his friends, he shouted, "The weird girl just asked me to dance," his voice echoing off the walls and ceiling.

Lola is a great dancer. After she gave up on disciplining me, right before she had her accident, she tried to teach me to dance. She would balance a big pile of dusty vinyl disks on the spindle of an ancient record player, and as they dropped one by one, she'd demonstrate a new step. At first I was too embarrassed to try, so she just danced alone.

"Rhumba," she'd shout and go careening away, her feet gliding across the freshly husked floors. If one of the maids happened into the room, she'd become Lola's partner. And then it was, "One-two-cha-cha-cha! Mambo, Swing, Jitterbug, Electric Glide, Boogie Woogie, Mazurka, Habanera, Fandango, Salsa, Merengue, Twist, Waltz, Samba, and the Tango," for my lola is not discriminating.

I danced with Lola three times before she had her accident. She said I was a natural. Maybe because I'd spent so many years doing gymnastics, the steps came easily. The first two times through a new dance I'd have to concentrate. Afterwards, we were free to talk.

When she was dancing, Lola never mentioned God, the Holy Virgin, or the wounds of martyrs. Instead, she talked about love. She told me how she'd met my grandfather at a dance—and how she wished she'd never danced with him. She blamed herself for my parents' marriage. "I think it's my fault that your mother fell for your father," she said. "I've always loved Italian and Spanish men. Imagine waltzing with Frank Sinatra or doing the tango with Marcello Mastroianni." Once, when she was teaching me to fandango, she whispered in my ear, "I love you, Antonio Banderas."

I was standing there, spacing out, thinking about Lola, when Malacoda grabbed me by the arm and guided me to the center of the room. "Arise ho to dance, oh thrice feted strumpet. Yea, though thou art possessed of tender quills, hope hath no more beloved notion than that which the dancer dancing may tread upon. Arise ho, I say, and dance the hey nonny, nonny dance!"

Suddenly there was a line of men standing in front of me, all of them dressed in tuxedos or antique military uniforms with medals and ribbons and upholstery fringe on their shoulders. I looked for Fra Umberto. He was still standing by the entrance, a Viking on either side of him. His head was bowed, his hands were joined on his belly, and it seemed his lips were moving. If I hadn't known better, I would have guessed that the old phony was praying. Once again, when I needed him most, I was on my own.

First in line was Christian Slater. He was wearing this incredibly cute white uniform that was tight in all the right places. But his make-up was really thick. It looked like someone had gone crazy with the foundation, wadding it on with a trowel. I had the impression that I could reach out and mold his face like it was made of play-dough. I know that most girls would die for the chance to dance with him, but I was afraid that his face might rub against mine, and then I'd probably throw up.

Andre Agassi was next in line. He had a row of sweat beads on his forehead and another one right above his upper lip. What if he tried to kiss me?

I turned down Michael Jordan, Elvis, Ringo Starr and Jimi Hendrix, John F. Kennedy, Denzel Washington, Michael Chang, Keanu Reeves and Pete Sampras; all of Lola's heart-throbs; the poet Catullus, escaped from the wax museum, who whispered a filthy limerick in my ear; Alcibiades, who offered to burn a goat for me; Brad Pitt, who offered to burn a dog; Muhammad Ali and David Robinson; the Lee brothers, Bruce and Spike; Dennis Hopper, Casanova, Alberts Einstein and Camus, Kurt Cobain, Fred Astaire, David Wu, Achilles, and Paris, who offered me a golden apple.

After I'd turned down several dozen offers, Malacoda and her Viking friends started getting restless. Anytime I rejected someone they went after him, whacking him on the back and thighs with their wiffle ball bats. I don't know why they were so interested in having me dance. But it gave me the creeps. I decided I wouldn't dance no matter who asked. Anyway, they were all grown men, and I couldn't understand why they would want to dance with me.

Next in line was Kevin Costner, who kept looking over his shoulder as if he wanted to examine the way his pants fit his behind. I was checking the same when I saw that Bri was next in line. I was suspicious, of course. So far, every time I thought I'd seen him it had turned out to be someone else. I didn't say anything. I let him walk up to me.

Everything about him was perfect. The hair had just the right mix of brown, yellow, and black strands. The mole on his left nostril stood out like an apostrophe. Only his eyes seemed a bit strange: the color was right, but something else seemed to be missing.

"Would you like to dance?" Bri said, with the cutest Danish accent.

"Yes," I said, though I didn't believe he was Bri.

He took a tentative step towards me, but he didn't raise his hands. Maybe it was because he was nervous. Maybe he didn't know what to do. When finally we locked fingers, I lost the ability to breathe. Now I'll die, I thought. Now I'll die.

But this Bri was not a good dancer. He counted out loud and kept looking at his feet. Even waltzing, he stumbled after my lead instead of taking it himself.

That didn't make sense. I knew that Bri had taken dance lessons as a child in Denmark. He didn't like dancing, but he knew how to dance.

"You're not Bri, are you?" I said.

"Yes, I am," he protested.

But then his voice changed and so did his face. He grew taller and fatter. He became my stepfather.

I tried to pull away, but he was much too strong. I looked around for Fra Umberto. He was still standing by the doorway with the Vikings, his head piously bowed. The room seemed to grow smaller and darker. The music changed to an old slow swing number, Frank Sinatra.

Singing under his breath, humming now and then because he didn't really know the words, my stepfather danced an old man's stumbling two-step.

"I've got you under my skin," he droned. "Oo, oo, doo-doo, oh baby."

I looked at him again. The pink collar of his shirt was frayed. His lips were chapped. He was my father, not my stepfather.

He held my right hand so tightly that my fingers began to tingle. The music was torture: the tired violins, the menacing 4/4 swing beat, the cloying lyrics and corny timing. His breath smelled of pay phones and depression, a mixture of peanut butter and stale cigarettes. We danced to "Someone to Watch Over Me," "Old Man River," "Night and Day," "My Way," "Time After Time," "Dancing in the Dark." I thought I was going to scream when the disco version of "Strangers in the Night" began playing, and he got frisky, twirling me around under his arm.

To make matters worse, when he wasn't singing or humming he was talking. It wasn't a conversation. He didn't ask me any questions. He wasn't even apologizing or explaining anything. He was just telling stories the way he always did.

"When I was a kid growing up," he said, as if there was any other kind of kid, "my father put speakers in every room. He wanted to be sure that he could listen to Frankie even when he was on the can. I left home to get away from that. It was like big brother watching you wherever you went. You couldn't think without getting those lyrics all tangled up in your thoughts. But it's the strangest thing, now that I see you all grown up, or almost all grown up, I feel myself coming full circle." Then he began to dip his hips and croon, "Strangers in the night…"

When I knew him, my father had a good voice. He loved Mozart and Prince. He would sing old Italian songs that made me and my mother laugh. His voice was like a chuckle that threatened to go out of control. He hated Frank Sinatra. He made fun of Frank Sinatra: using a cucumber for a microphone, he would sway across the kitchen as if it was a stage.

"I know it hasn't been easy for you, moving around like this. Your mother and I worry about you..." But as he spoke, he began to tap dance, as if it was an old routine: Shuffle, hop-step. Shuffle, hop-step. "You could say I wanted to spare you what I went through. But the real truth is..." Now the dance changed, it was something Latin, three steps toward me, two back, his palms weaving with the music, his hand reaching for me, pulling me close and then, with a twirl, "I'm an adventurer!" he announced. "I can't stand to stay in one place for too long."

When he was done talking, the music stopped as if on cue. He let go of me, and I would have run if I hadn't been so confused. Instead, I just stood there watching him pat the pockets of his jacket as if he were looking for something.

"I know I have it somewhere," he said. And then he pulled from his shirt pocket a tiny blue horse made of Murano glass. "This is for you," he said, standing it in the palm of his hand, just as he had done when he'd given it to me for my seventh birthday. I remembered thinking it miraculous that the horse could stand as it did on two hooves the size of pins, mid-gallop, perfectly balanced.

I was tempted to take it, but I knocked it out of his hand instead. It shattered on the floor.

"You can't give me something I already have," I said.

CHAPTER TWENTY-FIVE

While my father was picking at a pimple on his chin, trying to think of something to say to me, I ran away. I had no idea where I was going. I didn't really believe that I could escape from the Vikings, but I had no intention of dancing with my father again.

Now that my hands were free, I thought about getting out, just plucking off my headgear, but that seemed useless. I'd been in Dløn for more than twenty-four hours. That was the longest time I'd ever spent in any environment. I was too proud to quit before I'd done what I'd set out to do. Anyway, there was nothing for me to do in my room except to talk to the walls and count the bars on my windows. If I'd had a project or an idea for a project, I might have jacked out. But I didn't have anything like that. I didn't even have any good books around. I'd finished everything that I'd borrowed from the library at the start of vacation. Friends weren't an option: I had none. It was pathetic. I knew it was. As for Lola, I only gave her one ten-minute visit a day. And then she hardly opened her eyes to acknowledge me. She'd just hold my hand and make me pray.

She'd take her rosary beads and show me the inscription: *Roma*.

She'd hold my hand like a needy child.

"See," she'd whisper, in a wheezy flail that I could barely recognize, this withering of her voice, her loud, nasty nasality replaced by this insect, this pneumonic snort of an ant.

177

"If you turn the word over, it becomes *amor. Roma; amor. Roma; amor. Roma; amor.*"

The senility of this repetition repulsed me. I would flee her room.

She was sick. She used to love to dance; now she could hardly move in bed. The jeepney driver who had bumped her came off with barely a scratch. She had refused to prosecute him, saying, upright above her covers, surrounded by candles and her images of the book of Hours and of her daughter, my mother, "It is fate."

When she exhibited this compassion, I knew that her mind was going.

At first, I thought it had been heroic, how she had refused to have the pins put in her tibia, or her humerus, or whatever it was the doctors had said. My grandmother, after all, is not a heroine's child for nothing, a survivor of wars and tax investigators, a woman to account for.

"What? Pins in my sockets? Metal tubes sticking in my bones? They may as well drive nails into my coffin! And anyway, why should I trust them, those doctors? They are men like your father. They want me to become like them, confabulated creatures, inhuman matter, metal springs without souls. People without a God! I will heal without becoming a magnet attractor, a pile of metallic junk. God will provide!"

And she stuck to her bed, speaking her prayers aloud in a mawkish torpor. Sometimes, I wondered if they were prayers. Sometimes I heard strange words, awful and idiotic codes that I recognized at some moments. Misericordia. The Rime of the Ancient Mariner. Hey nonny, nonny. Glory be to the Father, to the Son and to the holy hronir. Amen. I heard weird whispers wafting from her room.

Strangely enough, my grandmother seemed to grow stronger in her bed, her commands more ruthless, though trembly, her limbs rustling and flexing beneath her sheets, to the astonishment of her doctor, who still came in to see her, despite her orders.

"See," she would sneer, like a grasshopper munching, "and you wanted to put hangers in my skin. *Verguenza!*"

And he'd feel her firm, tangible tibia, her smooth shell.

We stopped dancing, though sometimes, when I peeked into her room, I thought she was looking at me. I didn't know whose affection she was measuring, hers or mine.

The last time I had visited, before she had locked herself into her room, she had crooked her arms toward me in an awkward way, because her shoulder was broken. It was an odd movement and frozen gesture. She sat up in her bed and lifted her left arm, so that it seemed to span a nonexistent torso. It was the gesture of the queens of Egypt, who held on to their men in the ritual of the weighing of the hearts, when the king's heavy deeds were balanced against the feather of truth. So the queens held their beloved, their dead king, in that iconic gesture of consolation my grandmother now adopted, because she couldn't stretch the fractured limb.

In that eerie posture, she beckoned me to her side. But she looked so odd there, crooked and discomposed, that I ran. Fleeing that air embrace, I found myself crying outside her room.

It was a strange sensation, this solitary breakdown. I never cried. Even when my mother told me my father would never come back—at least not to live, not to be with us in the house—I had just shrugged my shoulders. I remember saying to her, "How are you going to get to the mall?"

My mother didn't drive.

That morning, outside Lola's room, staring at a world that hadn't changed—the hangings and shelves in the hall, the wooden, lilting chimes above my head—while my grandmother lay with broken bones, muttering dangerously, and healing with words, I couldn't even tell you why I cried.

Anyway, I had heard them all already, her stories; an old lady's mad, sentimental cycle of regret.

I hated myself for my tears.

The maids, with excellent reason, hated me. If I walked into a room, they walked out. They wouldn't even watch TV with me. It didn't matter if their favorite show was on; if I came downstairs, they scuttled back into their holes.

If I had forced the issue, I could probably have gotten them to take me out. But unless you're a shopping freak like my mother, there's nowhere to go in this city. They've cut down all the trees, and they just keep on building more skyscrapers. From my window, looking south, all I see is a great big wall of cement, limestone, and glass. It's gotten so bad that they're endangering the durian crop.

Durian flowers blossom at night. I've never actually smelled them, but Lola says the scent is enchanting, as sweet as the fruit but without the rotten cheese stench to get through. Lola says if you breathe the perfume of durian blossoms too deeply you go crazy for a while. You have strange dreams. I'd like to try.

Anyway, like most night flowers in Mindanao, the durian is pollinated by bats. They're not any old bats. They're giant bats, with bodies like foxes and wing spans like hawks. These bats can only live in limestone caves. But for fifty years now they've been quarrying the limestone like crazy to build skyscrapers. Pretty soon, all the bats will be gone. It's amazing how things are connected. Sometimes, it seems that everything in the world is connected except for me.

It was funny when the Vikings tried to chase me. They were slow and awkward. They kept falling off their heels and crashing into one another. Malacoda was no better. Flailing with her whip and shouting orders, she kept getting in their way.

Whenever they ran into her, instead of helping them get up, she began cursing and beating them.

I ran around the room three times before I found the staircase. Descending into a hole in the floor in a gloomy corner of the room, it was a metal spiral just like the one we'd used to enter Dløn in the first place. I didn't use it right away because I was still worried about Fra Umberto. It occurred to me that if I got the Vikings who were guarding him to chase me he might escape in the confusion. Standing in front them, just far enough away so they couldn't reach out and grab me, I stopped, stuck out my tongue and shouted the only Old Norse insult I could remember, "You're the wives of trolls every ninth night!"

This made them furious. They started grunting and hissing, sticking their tongues out at me. Only once their tongues were out of their mouths, they couldn't get them back in. And these were tongues unlike any tongues I'd ever seen: huge and red, big bloody slabs of steak, covered with glistening saliva.

"Glub, glub!" shouted the two Vikings who'd been guarding Fra Umberto as they came after me. Their attempts were pathetic. They couldn't see to follow me because their tongues kept bouncing up and slapping their faces.

When she noticed the two Vikings with waggling tongues, Malacoda went nuts. She gave the order for the rest of the Vikings to attack the unlucky twosome, and pretty soon all of the Vikings were brawling, swatting each other with bats and rolling around on the floor. In the midst of the confusion, I took Fra Umberto's hand and we walked to the staircase.

This time, since we were descending, Fra Umberto went first. We'd been going for several minutes before I spoke. Much as I hated to admit it, I'd missed the old monk, and I wanted to know what he was thinking.

"I was pretty frightened," I said. "I thought that Malacoda and the Vikings were really going to hurt you."

"You're right," puffed the monk. "They were."

"But why? How? I mean, otherwise they seemed so ridiculous."

"There is nothing more dangerous than that which seems ridiculous."

That sounded both wise and stupid. I wondered if it was the sort of advice you could apply to life in general. No doubt that was what made my mother so dangerous. Anyone who would stay with my stepfather for as long as she has must be a menace. If I were married to a guy who messed around as much as he does, I'd kill him. But as long as she has money for shopping, my mother doesn't care what he does. I swear she's brain dead. She spends all her time buying shoes and surfing the Hairnet. She gets excited if she finds a new shade of lip gloss. She's more ridiculous than the stupid Vikings.

"I almost gave up," I told Fra Umberto.

"I know."

I couldn't see him. There was no light at all on the staircase. I could hear his footfalls and his breathing. And there was something reassuring about that.

"How do you know?" I said.

"I almost gave up, too."

"I was going to jack out."

"Maybe that's what you should do," he said.

"What would happen then?"

"If you're lucky, you might crash Dløn."

"And if I crashed Dløn, where would that leave you?"

"It wouldn't leave me anywhere."

"I wouldn't want to do that."

"It's all right. It's not as if I would feel anything." I could hear him breathing hard and heavy like an old man.

I felt so confused I almost cried.

"What about Apeiron?" I said when I'd recovered. "Couldn't you go back to Apeiron?"

"No," he said in a muffled voice. "Apeiron is gone."

"I'm sorry," I said. I felt terrible. Even in virtual reality I was always hurting the wrong people. "Is there anything we can do?"

"Doubtful."

"What happened?"

"Dløn."

"So what is it? What is Dløn?"

"A tremendous mess. Somebody's idea of a joke."

"Who do you think is responsible?"

"Somebody or something deeply ridiculous, and deeply troubling."

"I almost don't care about finding Bri anymore," I said. "If I had something to do outside, and if I wasn't worried about you…"

"I'm touched, but your emotions are misplaced. You really shouldn't form an attachment to me. I don't even exist. Everything worthwhile is out there. If I were you, I'd jack out now," he said, pausing to catch his breath. "No, if I were you, I would have stayed out to start with."

I hated it when he said things like that. In a way, he was more substantial than anyone else I knew. In a way, he was my only friend. I changed the subject. "I've seen several characters who looked like Bri, but then when I looked closer none of them turned out to be him."

"That means you're on the right track."

"Why?"

"It's a strategy. You're being lured. Someone wants you to keep coming."

"But I don't understand what the point is. I don't even know where I'm going or how I'm supposed to get there."

"And that still bothers you?"

"I'd like to understand."

Fra Umberto laughed. Then we continued to descend in silence.

Eventually, the stairway led us into a poorly lighted room that smelled vaguely of wet wool and candy. There was a lot of noise, excited voices, metal rattling, and hard ticking sounds, as if someone were banging on the walls with silverware. Once my eyes adjusted to the light, I saw that the room was crowded with children. Most of them were sitting on benches, bent over, lacing up ice skates. The ones who had finished were making their way to the far end of the room, wobbling on their skates, which made a ticking sound on the hard plastic floors.

CHAPTER TWENTY-SIX

One little girl was sitting by herself on a bench, trying un-successfully to lace her skates. Something about the way she pursed her lips, a cute, concentrated crookedness, reminded me of my mother. She was about four years old, and she had perfect little fingers. Even though it was obvious that she could sit there until her fifth birthday and never get it right, she did not seem the least bit impatient. She could loop the laces over the hooks without too much trouble, but when it came to tightening, she would let go of the ends for a moment, and then all of her work would be for nothing.

I sat down next to her and watched for several minutes. When I said "Hello," she did not even look up from her skates. They were the same cheap red plastic things that all of the other girls were wearing. Boys had black.

I couldn't believe that a skating rink in Dløn would en-force such a stupid rule. I swore that if I went skating, I would wear black skates. I didn't care if it meant stealing them from another kid.

"Are you a clown?" the little girl mumbled without look-ing up from her skates.

I had forgotten that I was still wearing the stupid Hron outfit. I wondered what the make-up looked like after my swim in the trough. Maybe it was a good sign that I still looked like a clown.

"No," I said, "although certain people have been trying to make me into one."

"Good," she said. "Nene doesn't like clowns."

Nene was short for Nemencia. My lola still called her Nene. All of my cousins called her Tita Nene. I just called her Mom.

"Mom?" I said, and then I caught myself. "You're Nene?"

She stopped messing with her laces and looked at me. "Why did you call me Mom? I'm just a little girl. You're a big girl, and I'm just a little girl. I can't be a mom."

It was weird to watch her. She twitched her nose and squinted exactly the way my mother does when she's skeptical about something. "I know," I mumbled. "I don't know what I was thinking. It's just that you remind me of my mom."

"Is your mom a little girl?"

I nodded. In a way, my mom is a little girl. That's probably why she's afraid to be around me. She hates to be reminded of her responsibilities.

"Do you want me to help you with your skates?"

"Nene do it herself," she said, sticking her chin out.

"I'll only help you with the last bit," I said. "You lace them. I'll tie them."

Now Fra Umberto appeared, grinning and holding up two pairs of skates, one huge black pair and a red pair, apparently for me.

"What size?" I said.

"Five," he said.

"That's right," I said. "But I won't wear them."

"Why not?"

"I want black ones."

"The black ones are for boys."

"I don't care," I said. "I want black."

"Nene wants black, too," Nene said, kicking off one of her skates.

"Now look what you've done," said the priest.

"I don't care," I said. "I'm not going skating unless you get me black ones."

Nene kicked off the other skate. Fra Umberto picked up Nene's skates and walked back over to wait in line.

"I'm going to be your daughter when you grow up," I said to Nene just to see how she would respond.

Nene started crying.

I patted her on the leg. "Why are you crying, Nene?"

"Nene doesn't want a clown baby."

I took the hem of my costume and tried to wipe some of the greasepaint off of my face.

"I'm not really a clown," I said.

"Nene already has babies, twenty-five hundred, a million babies," Nene said, spreading her arms as if to indicate just how many babies she had.

"Where are your babies, Nene?" I asked.

"Nene's babies are everywhere," she said. "All of the babies are Nene's babies."

"All of the children here?"

"Everywhere."

"Am I your baby?"

Nene didn't answer. She looked at her feet and wiggled her toes. "Nene has blue socks," she said. "What color socks do you have?"

I had no idea. My socks were hidden in the folds of my floppy clown pants. I had to dig to find them. When I finally uncovered them, I discovered they were blue, too.

Nene was so excited by the discovery she screamed.

"All of Nene's children have blue socks," she announced.

After several minutes Fra Umberto came back with three pairs of black skates. He put his on in a flash, and then he helped Nene with hers. She didn't seem to mind that he helped her. Mine were a bit tight, but I wasn't going to complain. I knew that Fra Umberto had been through a lot lately.

Fra Umberto was easily the best skater I have ever seen. If he were to enter the Olympics, he would take every medal, whether it was for figure skating, hockey, or speed skating. He was just as fast backwards as he was forwards. With his black habit billowing about him, he looked like a cross between an obese bat and a strange acrobatic frog. He did leaps and loops and effortless triple lutzes, axles, and salkows. He even did a back flip that made his habit pop up over his head. Doing that, he reminded me of my grandmother, twirling and twirling as she danced. He even had her puckering features as he made a swift turn, the way Lola, when she concentrated, turned out her lower lip, and the skin about her dreamy brown eyes wizened. And he was as graceful as my lola.

At first I was so amazed that I couldn't do anything but stand there admiring his performance. But gradually I began to get annoyed with him. There was something obscene about a priest who was so accomplished at such a mundane activity. In my lola, grace seemed a matter of natural order: dancing was part and parcel of a Filipino childhood, the lovely evolution of a girl. As for Fra Umberto, in order to get so good, he must have spent an ungodly number of hours practicing. Anyway, it bugged me that he was so absorbed in something that obviously wasn't bringing us any closer to solving our problems.

Mostly I was annoyed because I was stuck with Nene who couldn't skate at all. She kept catching her tips on the ice and falling. The first few times she took me with her. Once I fell hard and twisted my wrist.

I'm not a great skater, but I'm not bad either. I don't know any tricks, unless you count skating backwards. I'm fast though. I can keep up with almost anybody, and I hardly ever fall. But I was afraid to leave Nene. We stayed close to the walls, so that we would have something to grab onto if we stumbled.

Since we were skating so slowly, I had plenty of time to examine the place. It seemed that we were at the bottom of the atrium. Actually, there was still no way to tell for certain which way was up and which way was down. It was like being inside a polyhedron in which every wall has its own gravitational force. If I was standing at the bottom, then the Barbies, five hundred meters up, appeared to be hanging upside down from their giant cement trees. The hallway with the Hronic classrooms in it was about forty meters up, jutting through a wall at a vertiginous acute angle, so that the clowns appeared to be walking up and down a ski-slope. The mist that I had noticed before was steam rising from the ice. The ant-like things darting back and forth were the skaters.

Examining Dløn from this perspective, I realized that Dløn's architect had borrowed heavily from Hypermall, Southeast Asia's largest mall, the hangout of all the coolest kids at school. Just like Hypermall, Dløn had a skating arena at the center. Only this one was huge. It was so big and so crowded that I could not see the other end. Instead of the pop songs that blare out from the speakers at Hypermall, this rink had an old electric organ that kept playing the same cheesy waltzes and marches over and over again.

The ice was strange. It had images of people embedded in it. They were so lifelike, you would have sworn that they were really there, frozen into the ice. All of them were children, and all of them wore skates. They were packed so densely that unless you stopped and looked closely, you couldn't really pick out any individual features. I examined one boy who had an astonished look on his face, like he never knew what had hit him.

We'd been skating for about half an hour when we spotted the Zamboni. Actually, we heard it first. It sounded like a combination tractor and slush-cone machine. At every skating rink I've ever visited, they clear the people off before they bring on the Zamboni. Here, the thing just plowed right through the crowd, knocking over anyone who happened to get in the way.

Maybe because they were so surprised that they didn't have time to get scared, none of the children screamed when they were run over. The Zamboni operated with ruthless efficiency. It swallowed any skaters who happened to be in its way, leaving a trail of wet ice over the newly embedded children. Out of the exhaust pipe—a giant tube mounted right behind the cab—the Zamboni spewed the strange disembodied signs that floated up into the atrium. From this perspective, they looked even less substantial. In fact, they were just smoke puffs with peculiar shapes.

If you paid attention, it was pretty easy to predict where the Zamboni was going. It didn't seem to chase anybody. It just ran down anyone who got in its way. Fra Umberto was such a confident skater that he would cut right in front of it if that happened to fit with his routine. He didn't seem to notice what the Zamboni was doing, or if he did, he didn't seem to care.

In the meantime, kids just kept streaming onto the ice, so it never really got any less crowded. If anything, I had the sense that it was getting more crowded. Every now and then it would get so thick that you could hardly move. In certain places along the wall, older kids, mostly girls in tight jeans and stylish sweatshirts, gathered to talk. When the little kids who were holding the wall ran into these clumps it caused major problems. Inevitably, someone would fall down and drag a whole group with them.

I was trying to get around one of these clumps when the Zamboni snuck up on us. I don't remember how it happened. All I know is that one second I was holding Nene's sweaty little hand and then I wasn't. Somehow she had wiggled loose at just the wrong moment and had skated right out in front of the Zamboni.

I could hardly bear to look. When I did, the resemblance to my mother was even more uncanny. Frozen in the ice, she looked exactly like a photograph that Lola has in her room. She was lying on her side. Her mouth was open as if she'd tried to say something.

I wanted to cry but I couldn't. I sat down on the ice, put my hands over my head and tried. But nothing came out. It was like something hard and heavy had lodged itself in my heart. I wanted it out, but I was also afraid that if I let it go, I would never get it back. It would just float around like those letters in the atrium where anyone could grab it and use it against me later.

I hated the evil things that kept happening here. I didn't care if Nene wasn't a real child. I just hated it. It was so stupid and senseless. Her hand had felt like a real child's hand. Her voice had sounded like a real child's voice. She was funny and cute, and she looked like my mother.

When I stood up, I was furious. If this was another sign that I was on the right track then I didn't want to be on the right track. I wanted to get off of it. I looked around for Fra Umberto. He was still pirouetting about like nothing at all had happened.

I took off after the Zamboni. I decided I would get the bastard who had run down the children or I would die trying.

CHAPTER TWENTY-SEVEN

The Zamboni was not moving all that fast. Once I made up my mind, it was easy enough to catch it. I don't think anyone inside noticed me because the Zamboni didn't speed up or start swerving or anything.

On my rollerblades, I've caught rides behind trucks, buses, and cars; when they notice you, they do all kinds of sick things. They accelerate over speed bumps. They try to run you into the curb, a sewer, or a street sign. The Zamboni just kept chugging along at the same slow, systematic pace, as if running over children was as ordinary as plowing a street after a snow storm.

I had some trouble climbing onto the Zamboni. The platform at the back was about two meters up, and there was no ladder. I had to let go of the under-chassis and jump to reach the platform. It occurred to me that Fra Umberto could have done it easily, but I didn't want his help. I wasn't sure if I could trust him. He wasn't the same Fra Umberto. He had lost his anger, his sense of purpose.

The first time I tried to get up onto the platform, I didn't even get close. I wiped out on top of a pile of freshly frozen kids. It occurred to me that I needed to build up some momentum before I jumped. Twice I tried skating and jumping. And twice I went on my face.

On the third try I caught the platform, but my right skate got hooked on the under-chassis. I knew if I fell, I would slam my head. I squirmed and pulled with all my might. Finally, with one lucky kick, I freed my blade and heaved myself onto the platform. It was a metal grating, impossible to walk on with skates. I took my skates off, tied the laces together, and slung them around my neck.

Smoke from the chimney stung my nostrils. The organ was pounding out a patriotic march. I felt it right between my eyes. It was disorienting. For a moment I couldn't remember what I was doing.

The door at the end of the platform opened into a hot, dark, cramped space. There was a sound like paper rustling; here the smoke was more acrid than ever. It took me a while to adjust to the lighting. The room was filled with *duwendes* —precisely as Lola had described them: tiny people, no bigger than my thumb. There were hundreds, maybe thousands of them. Some, working with little scissors, were cutting the words out of books. Others seemed to be sorting and stacking the words. But by far the largest number were shoveling huge heaps of words into a great potbellied furnace. I don't know if this furnace actually powered the Zamboni, but I have no doubt that it produced the smoky letters that floated about in the atrium.

It was too dark and too smoky for me to distinguish any of the words that the *duwendes* were handling. I realized that this was the first writing—apart from the illegible newspapers in my grandfather's shop—that I'd seen anywhere in Dløn. And I became desperate to read something, even if it was only one word.

Knowing that I needed the *duwendes'* cooperation, I decided to follow Lola's instructions to the letter. If she'd been right about the *tikbalang,* she must've known what she was talking about.

I bent down before a group of *duwendes* that was busy with the vivisection of a beautiful folio volume of poetry. The paper was iridescent, white and crisp, like that of the books that filled Dr. Jack's shelves. I desperately wanted to hold it.

I cleared my throat and spoke as politely as possible, using every term of respect I could think of. "If you please, honorable *duwendes,* I hope that I would not offend you if I asked permission to glance for a moment at one of the words in the book."

None of the *duwendes* looked up from their work. None of them spoke in answer. They continued working as if they had not heard me, but just as I was about to clear my throat and try again, my eyes stinging so much I was sure I was going to cry, I felt something brush my left hand.

It was lovely paper, rough and crisp. I imagined that I could smell the ink, the sweet sans-serif typeface. At first, when I could not read what was written on the paper, I was angry. I felt that I was being cheated again—that this was another trick like the false Bris and Fra Umberto's promises.

But I did not give up immediately. I kept tilting the paper and turning it until the light from the furnace fell at just the right angle. There was a word on the paper, and I read the word.

I do not think that *duwendes* can read. I do not think that they chose that particular word. I don't think it matters what the word was. It was a word, and I read it.

CHAPTER TWENTY-EIGHT

For a moment after I read the word, it seemed that everything around me came to a halt, like the pause that punctuates the movements of a concerto, so brutally clean, long, and quiet you feel like screaming. But I did not scream, and the *duwendes* went on working, ignoring me entirely. Only now I noticed that they were tied together in groups of eight or ten with ropes as thin as a spider's web. Although the ropes were thin, they were apparently effective, because I didn't see a single *duwende* struggle to get free. They merely continued with their work as if they had no choice at all.

I was trying to figure out why they didn't just run off when I noticed the beast who was guarding them. He was lying in a corner in front of a door, licking his fur with one of his tongues, panting and drooling from another mouth, and growling through the teeth of a third.

I don't like dogs. They smell bad. They're foolish. They're loyal to people who don't deserve loyalty. This dog was particularly foul—long-legged, gaunt, and mean-looking, the kind of dog that never approaches you directly but circles, trying to sneak up and take a chunk out of your behind.

I knew that the door he was guarding led to the control room of the Zamboni, and I wanted to get inside. The dog knew this too. His laziness was his strength. Lying in front of the door, he could watch the *duwendes* and block my progress without ever taking a break from licking himself.

I'm not one of those people who hate dogs out of fear. I'm not the least bit afraid of them. Dogs view the world simplistically. They prey on those who are weaker; they bow before those who are stronger. If you behave like the top dog, other dogs will do what you want them to: they'll even chase their own tails.

I walked right up to him and called him puppy. When he growled, I shushed him. Finally, I used my skates to undo him. I held the laces so one of the skates spun above his heads. He stopped licking himself and began to whimper. All six eyes became focused on the spinning blade. Suddenly, I jerked the spinning skate back towards his tail, taking care to keep it out of his reach. His left head twisted to the left; the right one spun to the right. He barked and leaped at the skate, trying to catch it with all three mouths at once, and landed whimpering, sprawled on his belly.

The door swung open, and a giant figure filled it almost entirely. I recognized the beard immediately. I'd seen it a thousand times in the mirror. It was Fergus.

"Don't tease the dog," he growled.

The only thing worse than dogs are the people who own dogs. They treat them like children. They spend all their money on them, and they talk about them constantly, as if they were children. My mother has a dog now—a little yappy thing. My stepfather gave it to her. It's supposed to be a comfort, now that I'm away. I know that I have never been a comfort to anyone. I certainly had no intention of being a comfort to Fergus.

"He was blocking my way."

"That's his job."

I laughed.

The dog whimpered and nuzzled one of his heads against Fergus's leg. Fergus moved to the side, holding the dog by the collar. "Well, come on then," he said. "Come on inside."

The Zamboni's control room reminded me of the bridge of the Starship Enterprise. A dozen geeky technicians sat in front of consoles, spinning trackballs and tapping away at keyboards. The walls were covered with blinking lights, monitors, and slots that spewed out reams of paper covered in hexadecimal code. On the far wall was a giant window overlooking the skating rink where Fra Umberto was still performing and children were still getting flattened.

Fergus walked with me to the middle of the room. He moved strangely, dragging his feet a bit, appearing to struggle. He was not entirely himself. In fact, from the waist down he was moving backwards. Actually, it seemed his spine had been twisted like a pipe cleaner, so that now the crack of his butt was perfectly aligned with his Adam's apple and the tip of his nose.

My shock at his appearance must have been obvious because he began explaining before I could say anything.

"For everything we gain, we sacrifice something," he said. "I'm not as pretty as I used to be, but I'm infinitely more powerful." He grinned. "Make yourself comfortable," he added, pointing at a swivel chair at the center of the room. "Can I get you anything? A glass of juice, a durian?"

I shook my head. I was beyond hunger now.

"I love durian," he said. He reached into a cabinet on one of the walls and pulled out a perfect fruit, spiky and fragrant.

I couldn't keep from laughing when he sat down backwards on the chair next to mine.

"Durian is nature's own fondue—fruit and cheese in one," he whispered, splitting the tough, spiny shell with his bare hands, peeling it as if it were an orange. The perfume was gripping. "This is Thai durian," he said. "Do you know how they ripen durian in Thailand?"

I ignored the question.

"They wrap the whole unripe fruit in grass and feed it to an elephant. The durian stays in the elephant's gut for days. The elephants can't digest it. Imagine trying to pass a durian." He grinned. "Finally, after the elephant squeezes it out, they harvest it from the dung heap. These durian are supposed to be the best durian of all, the most fragant, the most varied and subtle in their bouquet."

He spit a seed onto the floor, where it glistened like a great greasy cow's eye.

"Have some," he said, holding a handful of ripe pulp under my nose.

"No thanks."

"Are you afraid you'll be stuck here if you eat it?"

I didn't answer.

"Did the priest tell you that?"

"He might have."

"And you trust him?" He shook his head as if he was disappointed. "He's the one who made you travel here without armor or weapons of any kind. Imagine how much easier it would have been if you'd only had a laser, or even a good knife?"

"I'm looking for someone," I said.

"Haven't you figured it out yet?"

"What?"

Fergus turned into Bri. It wasn't the slow metamorphosis I was accustomed to. He changed instantly.

"Stay here," he said, and his voice was Bri's. "Be my queen and rule Dløn with me."

"You're not Bri," I said, although I wasn't sure.

"And you're not Leo. No one is himself or herself in Dløn. I am that I am, or I am that I am not. Here, we all take on disguises. We are disguises under disguises."

"Why are you running over those children?"

"Didn't you look at the ice?"

"I did."

"And didn't you find it beautiful?"

I shook my head.

"Haven't you understood at all? Dløn is a work of art. It's the war that I declared on you, and the poem that I composed for you. For you, those children are preserved forever in ice. What could be more beautiful?"

"Almost anything," I said.

He shook his head, and he looked miserable. "I know you've marveled at the effects of smart bombs. I know you've admired the pattern of guts spilled on a sidewalk, the spirals of smoke from a napalmed village. I know you're an artist, and I want you to paint me a picture. Run over the priest, and all of Dløn will be yours."

"Why would I want to stay in Dløn. Dløn is an awful place. Anyway, I like Fra Umberto. I like him better than I like you."

Bri held a fleshy chunk of durian to his lips, sucking quietly. He was even more beautiful than I remembered. His hair was tousled as if he had just been swimming. His eyes sparkled. He licked at his lips with an agile, pointed tongue. My comment didn't seem to bother him at all.

"Let me make it simple for you," he said. "You have two choices: either you run over the priest or you watch while I do."

"What has Fra Umberto done to you?"

"Nothing."

"Then why run him over?"

"Because I can. Because I want to."

"Do you think that's right?"

"Right or wrong, who cares? I do what I want here. This is my universe. And in my universe, my wishes are not only right, they're necessary and beautiful."

I felt betrayed. I don't trust many people. I'd thought that Bri was someone I understood. But it turned out he was as sick and cruel as Dløn itself.

I watched Fra Umberto again. And I felt even more miserable. He was no longer himself. The anger was gone, and so was the curiosity. Maybe Dløn had already destroyed him. He had protected me so many times, and now that he was about to be flattened, I couldn't think of any way to help him.

Then I had an idea.

"Before I do anything," I said. "You have to prove that you are Bri."

"How?"

"Recite a poem for me?"

"Which poem?"

"You have to ask?"

"You name it."

"Recite 'Who Goes with Fergus?'"

"Wait a second," he said. He giggled. He stammered. "Can you get me started?"

I watched Fra Umberto. Rushing across the ice, he looked as if nothing could hurt him. I had the sense that his every gesture was meant to tell me something. It was as if he was not skating but speaking. I had only to listen, and I would understand. Soon, his message became as clear as the great ski slope in the middle of my face.

"You're wrong about my choices," I said. I felt immense. I felt ecstatic. I hadn't written the poem in my journal. There had been no need. I knew it by heart. I had learned it by heart the first time I'd heard it. I recited:

Who will go ride with Fergus now,
and pierce the deep wood's woven shade,
and dance upon the level shore?
Young man, lift up your russet brow,
and lift your tender eyelids, maid,
And brood on hope and fear no more.

And no more turn aside and brood
on love's bitter mystery;
For Fergus rules the brazen cars,
And rules the shadows of the wood,
And the white breast of the dim sea
And all disheveled wandering stars.

I recited, and when I'd finished, I tore my headgear off.

CHAPTER TWENTY-NINE

The room was filled with gray light. The sun had not risen yet. There was a red swatch on the horizon. I had gone offline about two hours before I was supposed to.

The stench in the room was unbearable. There were bed sheets and books strewn all over the floor. Beneath my seat, a dozen durian seeds sat in a puddle the size of a beach towel. Three days ago, I would've thrown a fit. I would've roused the maids and forced them to clean up. Now, the thought of treating someone that way made me feel nauseous.

I found a sponge on the ridge of the bathtub, and I used it to mop the floor. It was slow work. My hands were shaking, and the walls seemed to be closing in on me. I felt dizzy. My tongue filled my mouth like a dry woolen mitten.

After I was done cleaning the room, I took a shower. I tilted my head back and drank the water. At first it hurt to swallow. But after a while I couldn't stop drinking.

I was drying off, leaning against the sink, when I decided to go for a walk outside. I had never been out of the house alone before. But I didn't think it would be too hard to sneak out. Everyone else was still asleep. I could see Emman, the guard, sprawled on the car, clutching his shotgun. It protruded from his chin like the snout of a *tikbalang*.

Not wanting to be conspicuous on the street, I brushed my hair and put on the first thing I clutched, a dress. The maids must have left it out on Lola's orders, for Easter Sunday Mass. It was the only dress I owned, a poofy yellow thing that Lola had given me right after I arrived. After trying it

205

on the first time, I had never worn it again. I didn't think. I put it on. I looked at myself in the mirror. I looked pale and stumpy, like an exhausted, elfin ballroom dancer. I smiled. It was the perfect disguise. I didn't look like myself. If the guards at the gate asked, I would tell them I was going to Mass.

I was on the landing, about to go downstairs when I felt the urge to see Lola. It was a stupid notion, almost self-destructive, but I couldn't help myself. Holding my shoes in my left hand, I shuffled back up the stairs and down the hallway to the back of the house to Lola's bedroom. I opened the door slowly, a centimeter at a time. The room was still dark. The only window faced west. I had to open the door all the way to see anything at all.

I was looking at the picture of my mother on the nightstand, remembering the way Nene's hand had felt in mine, when Lola turned in her bed, and I realized that she was not asleep.

"Amor," she said. Her suspicious brown eyes stared straight at me. I'd forgotten how imposing she could look, despite the wrinkles, her sallow illness—even if all you saw were her eyes. No wonder the maids were terrified. Her eyes pinned me like a magnet. "Come closer. You look beautiful."

I did what she told me. I went to her bed, I leaned over her, and I put her hand to my forehead. I could feel her veins through her cool, soft skin.

Her voice still had that altered burr, frail and snappish, but it didn't matter. She was as I remembered her, restless and alive. Her gnarled, nasty fingers twitched, held out to me. The hands that ordered her universe. Hands that danced the tango and embellished stories, hands that cupped and whispered songs. Hands that hailed, hands that held me. The only hands that caught me when we danced.

Maybe it was true: ladies like my grandmother can heal themselves. What Lola's stories had long ago taught me was this: Nothing is surprising.

Her hand was raised toward me like that, in that crooked gesture of an air embrace: that familiar pose. The gesture of the queens of Egypt. I knelt down and draped it against my shoulder, so that her broken, livid arm spanned my back and thus held me, in that awkward gesture of consolation. Her moist palm breathed against my skin.

Lola smiled. *"Amor,"* she slurred. "Where are you going all dressed up like that?"

I lied. "Lola," I said against her ear. "It's Easter Sunday. I'm going to Mass with Chuki and Miraflor."

Lola nodded. Her hair brushed against my cheek. "That's good. You spend too much time inside the house."

I could not see whether she was smiling, but I had that impression. She squeezed my shoulder and let me go. Then she rolled over and went back to sleep. I stood up. Hunched like that, her bedcovers over her, I had a strange notion, as if I recognized the bulk. A broad monkish habit thrown across her shoulders, so that her oddly scrunched side looked like a supine potbelly, a soccer ball jelly belly.

Part of me wanted to wake her up again, to tell her about my adventures. But the part of me that was wiser decided to let her sleep. What would I have told her?

I don't know who created Dløn or why they created it. I know it wasn't Bri, because Bri does not exist. More precisely, the Bri in Dløn was my invention. I was lonely. I wanted company, so I tried to create a friend. I cobbled him out of bits and pieces borrowed from other people. I took his mole and his eyes from a former teacher. His name and his accent belong to a classmate, but after I made fun of him he never spoke to me, not even electronically. The hair came from a boy I saw diving from a pier to retrieve coins in

Manila Bay. Everything else—his ideas, his pride, his cruelty—came from me.

I knew this when Fra Umberto asked me to travel with him to Dløn. I knew that it was not a question of rescuing a real person. I was not acting out of altruism. Just like my guide, I hoped to recover lost property, information that had been stolen from me: the journal that had disappeared from my hard drive. I was also looking for a new game, a better challenge. In my pride, I wanted to take on the entire network, the world.

I don't blame anyone else for the things that happened in Dløn. I misled myself. I devised my own tortures. But it would be arrogant to think that Dløn was created just to teach me a lesson. I don't know what it means or whether it has a purpose. I don't know who controls it. Fra Umberto was probably right—Dløn is whatever Dløn can get away with. It tries to separate you from yourself. But it didn't work with me. I'm just as much myself as I ever was.

I walked by Emman as if it was something I did every morning. The gate squeaked when I opened it, but he didn't budge. Although it was light now, no one was out on our street. I felt giddy walking away from the house. I tripped on a speed bump, and I almost fell over. The light hurt my eyes. I had been in VR so long that I had trouble blinking. Everything was brighter and harsher. The outlines of trees against the sky were unbearably precise.

As I approached the corner, I heard people talking. Two women were teasing each other about something in loud Visayan voices, their vowels rattling like money in a can.

When they saw me, they stopped talking. I tried to make eye contact with one of them. I nodded, but she just watched me through squinted eyes. Then, when my back was turned, they both broke into laughter, their voices rattling even louder, as if they were emptying the coins from the can. If I hadn't been so nervous, I might have gone back and given them a piece of my mind.

At the exit, the guard saluted and raised the gate for me to pass. I was about to step into the street when a horn sounded and an ancient taxi rattled by, passing so close I felt the heat of its exhaust on my legs.

I had never been this close to the world. All my life I had been pampered, left to the solitude of my devices, my mother's guilt-giving and my grandmother's tales. I had blamed everyone else for my strangeness, my belligerence and isolation, when all I had needed to do was step out.

Briefly, I remembered one last expression, the look on Fra Umberto's face as I had seen it from the Zamboni—as if it had been a message, a sign. His last wave: that crooked, almost misshapen gesture. The image dissolved of its own accord, like a feather tipped and falling, lost and forgotten as I moved.

Instead of crossing, I walked along the fence that separated the village from the world. The street was already busy. A giant yellow bus rumbled by, making the ground tremble. There were jeepneys, taxis, passenger cars, and pedicabs— all driving as if they were late for a wedding.

I had to walk carefully on the sidewalk. It had been torn up in places. There were bits of rubble, broken glass, and piles of sand every few paces. A candy wrapper catching the sunlight blinded me for a moment. I looked into a manhole that had no cover. There was a river running beneath the street. The stench was unbearable. It lingered for several minutes. I began to sweat. My knees went wobbly.

I stopped at the corner where the fence came to an end and leaned against a telephone pole. I could see the flicker of an arc welder's torch forty stories up in a new building. I tried to imagine what sort of life they led so many meters above the pavement.

Every day, all of this was going on without me. I could disappear at any moment and no one would notice. I did not feel sorry for myself. I knew that compared with most of the people who live in this city, I do not suffer at all. Every day new buildings are built here. Every day there are more buses, more cars, more jeepneys. People flock from the provinces hoping for better lives, only to find themselves living under bridges. Sewage flows to the river, the river empties into the bay. Sometimes it floods the streets. A million people go hungry. Every day a child slips from the hand that holds her.

I felt a wind on my face and tasted the salt of my own tears. I was alive. No virtual wind ever blew like this one. It carried the sounds of gongs and drums. I looked up a side street and coming my way was a procession of women and girls, hundreds and hundreds dressed in blue and yellow, playing gongs and banging on drums and dancing the wild dance of the full moon and vernal equinox. Leading them all was a woman in white, waving a huge bright banner.

Above the procession a flame tree was in bloom. Bright red petals were falling from the branches like snow in fiery flurries. The ground was covered in petals. The women had petals on their shoulders and in their hair.

All my life, I had been protected, but I would be no longer. Now that I was out in this mess, I intended to stay. When the procession reached the corner, the bells of Saint Andrew's began to ring as if they would never stop, and I stepped from the curb to join the dancers.

AFTERWORD

I met Arne at a cocktail party for graduate students—we were to be two of ten fiction writers in the Johns Hopkins program that year. My first impression of Arne: He was way too well-adjusted to be enrolled in any kind of arts program. He wore his hair bushy and sported a pair of aggressively out-of-fashion aviator glasses. He smiled. He circulated around the room shaking hands and fetching people drinks. Among the flagrantly neurotic chain smokers, Arne appeared to be a puffy cloud of goodwill and wholesomeness.

The truth was much more complicated, but I was not equipped at the time to appreciate that. Arne defied all those labels. He appeared to be nothing more complicated than a Mr. Nice Guy—but get him talking, and you'd find out he was a Harvard graduate working on an epic novel that ricocheted from Norse mythology to modern-day Denmark—laboring at this task while he held down a job as a high-school American history teacher. Deep in his brain, he was building cathedrals of fantasy and honeycombs of erudition.

One day I decided that I couldn't stand it anymore: all that secret coolness I'd glimpsed in Arne had to shine out. I decided the hair must go. At a party, I announced to Arne that I was giving him a cut.

"OK," he said cheerily, and sat down in a chair, without exhibiting any curiosity about the New Look I promised him. "Do you have any scissors?"

I lopped off hanks of chestnut hair, sculpting him into a Lyle Lovett, into a member of the Stray Cats, into a terribly hip art type. He looked fabulous, everyone at the party agreed, with his pompadour of curls. He glanced at himself in the mirror. "That's great," he said politely. And then he forgot about his hair, and it grew back bushy again.

After nine months at Hopkins, we all went our separate ways. Arne had fallen in love with another grad student writer, a woman from the Philippines named Gina. The first time they visited me in Boston, we sat in an underground cafe, thin winter light drizzling down on us. Even in that gloom, the two of them glowed. They'd just gotten married—on a windswept beach somewhere on Cape Cod, at the darkest time of the year. As they talked about the ceremony, I began to imagine how their clothes had whipped about their bodies, and the way the gray sand had shifted under their feet. How simple it had been and how stark.

They took whatever jobs they could get and devoted as much time as they could to writing. They sublet. They holed up indoors. They lived the dark and wintry existence of artists who are true to their art. Then they had a daughter, which changed things.

Next time I saw them, they were headed off to the Philippines, where they could live cheaply and more comfortably. They popped into town just as I was about to take the bus to the Cape. Arne and Gina offered to drive me down there, just so we'd have time to hang out.

Three writers and a baby on the highway: the adults discussed Borges and minimalism. The baby spoke in her own language. Pretty soon, we were good and lost. But not really lost, because we found ourselves at the exact same patch of beach where Arne and Gina had married. By now it was night. We stumbled out onto the sand and listened to the whoosh of water. Arne gestured around, showing me the place—as if there were something there to look at besides sand and black water. He talked again about the ceremony, how beautiful it had been. And I wished then I could glimpse whatever he wanted to show me here—perhaps the ghosts of himself and Gina, or the afterglow of a certain marbled sky.

They wrote me from the Philippines, where they'd both gotten jobs as teachers. Arne seemed delighted to be plunked down in another culture: He learned words in the native tongue; studied the mythology. He gushed about his students, the teen-aged mixed-race rich kids, so alike and so different from all the other kids he'd taught. He seemed determined to find ways to transmit his own delight in books to them, and was always in the process of inventing a new classroom project.

He and Gina spent several years out of the country, and I'd begun to feel like I'd lose track of them. Then suddenly, a phone call: They lived in New Hampshire now. Gina had gotten a fellowship at Exeter, which would allow both of them a year off to write.

I was in the process of buying a used car, and I consulted Arne frequently. Even if he penned fabulist novels and read Philippine ghost stories, he was also the kind of guy who knew what to look for in an aging Toyota. He was someone you could count on.

I went up to visit them at Exeter. He, Gina, and I went hiking in a forest in New Hampshire, and it was an odd repeat of the time we got lost in the Cape. We were talking so intently—about teaching, about introducing kids to high-tech, about the Web—that we paid no attention to our surroundings. Soon we found ourselves in a swamp, plodding through the mud, not sure which way to go. One of my last memories of Arne is his voice: He was off somewhere in the trees, scouting for a dry path, and he called to us. I can't remember what he said, only how I whipped my head around, expecting to see him. But he had turned invisible behind the locked arms of pine trees. He died ten days later.

213

He's still in my Rolodex. It's only about eight months ago that he died, and I feel so sick about it that I had to read this manuscript while I huddled under a quilt, a cup of tea beside me, as if I had the flu. I was mad at the manuscript, to tell you the truth. I was mad at it because, obnoxious and willful little thing, it found a publisher three weeks after Arne died. Why couldn't it have gotten itself accepted a little earlier? With its unruly pages spilling out across my lap, the manuscript seemed like a brat.

And yet, when I picked it up and began reading in earnest, I forgot how annoyed I had been. I forgot the steaming tea beside me and the rumbling of trucks outside. I was in its spell. This, I thought, is a fabulous book.

Leo@fergusrules.com reminds me of the novels I loved as a kid, Narnia, Alice, Phantom Tollbooth—books that are secret gardens, with pages that whisper of other worlds. And yet, because of its literary allusions (Borges, Eco, Dante et. al.) and challenging ideas, it definitely belongs in the adult section.

The narrator, a hormone-addled teen girl, dons a virtual-reality visor and goes off on a heroic journey that would make Joseph Campbell's head spin. On the way, she encounters mythological beasts from her Philippine grandmother's stories, a gaggle of mall rats, and a Zamboni ice-cleaner that's a portal to another dimension. *Leo@fergusrules.com* is a bit like a virtual-reality visor itself—disorienting, new, and utterly diverting. I wish that I could call up Arne and congratulate him on his triumph.

Pagan Kennedy
Somerville, Massachusetts
1999

THE AUTHOR

Arne Tangherlini received his A.B. in History and Literature from Harvard College and his M.A. from the Writing Seminars at Johns Hopkins University. He lived in Denmark, Italy and Manila. A teacher for many years both in the Philippines and the United States, he co-authored *Smart Kids: How Academic Talents are Nurtured and Developed in America.*